Courting a Christmas Wallflower

WALLFLOWERS AND ROGUES

CHRISTMAS WALLFLOWERS
BOOK TWO

DAWN BROWER

Courting a Christmas Wallflower

For all those that find strength when they need it most. Do not give up. You never know what you might discover in the middle of your journey.

You must be the best judge of your own
happiness.

— JANE AUSTEN, EMMA

Contents

EXCERPT: A WALLFLOWER UNDER THE MISTLETOE
DAWN BROWER

<h1 style="text-align:center">Prologue</h1>

Lightening flashed moments before thunder struck and rattled the windows of Evangeline Payne's bedroom. She shook beneath her blanket. Eva hated storms, but loud ones always made her especially nervous. This storm was no different.

Her mother, Daphne Atwood Payne, Viscountess Norwich had died during a storm like this one. That was four years earlier when Eva was three and ten. It was then when she'd become timid and lost the ability to speak well in polite company. Storms had become her greatest weakness.

Her father had changed after her mother's death too. He'd become distant and angry. His temper flared at the slightest provocation. Her stammer hadn't helped when he wanted her attention. She tried to avoid him at all costs. She relished the moments when she was allowed to visit her grandmother, Theodora, the Dowager Countess of Birchwood. At her grandmother's estate she felt free, but still even there with her three cousins for company she couldn't shake the stutter that plagued her.

She was going to stay with her grandmother in a week and she couldn't wait. The storm only made her more anxious. What if it was an omen of sorts? If her father forbade her from going Eva didn't know what she would do. She had to go. She just *had* to.

Eva slipped out of bed and made her way to the window. She should face her fear and maybe then she could lose the stutter too. Something had to change or she would never be able to escape her father's house. She needed to marry, and she prayed for something to help her do that.

Her hand shook as she opened the window. With it wide open wind blew inside and the rain pelted against her skin. She lifted her head and let it pour over her face. The pain that prickled her skin from the drops of water was enough to shock her to reality. *This was silly—what was she thinking?*. Another flash of lighting and the pound of thunder rattled around her. Eva took a deep breath and then stepped away from the window. Somehow, someway, she would have to shake herself free from the fear coursing through her. She was tired of being afraid.

She stared at the stormy sky and made a promise to herself. This summer when she was at her grandmother's estate, she would make a change. She would become a woman a man noticed, and she *would* find a husband. If she couldn't do that, then she had no real chance of a future. Her father drank too much brandy and he got meaner the more foxed he became. Her home had ceased being a place of safety once her mother had died.

Eva didn't want to be afraid of her own shadow anymore. It was time to live in the light. She stepped forward and closed the windows. Storms were not going to be her weakness anymore. Instead the tempest would be her strength as she walked into the storm and faced everything it threw her way.

She slipped into bed again and settled beneath

her blanket. For the first time in a long time she slept peacefully—fear no longer the curse that held her petrified. As if fate had given her a gift… One she had been waiting for and hadn't realized it. All she had to do was accept it and her greatest desire would be hers. *Finally*.

One

Eva stared out the window of the bedchamber she had been assigned at Seabury Castle. The castle was located along the shoreline, far outside of the village of St. Davids in Wales. It seemed almost as if her father had banished her to the ends of the earth, considering the castle's remote locale. After two failed seasons, her father had sent her to stay with her Aunt Clara, the Countess of Andover, who had found a husband in her first season. So somehow that made her the only person who could possibly help Eva find one herself.

It didn't matter to her father that Aunt Clara lived in such a remote location or that the chance Eva might meet a prospective husband would be unlikely. Eva believed her father had just wanted to send her away, and her lack of a successful season was an excuse to do so.

Aunt Clara had plenty of advice to give. Unfortunately, none of it was exceptionally useful to Eva. Her stutter made most gentlemen look upon her unfavorably, and no amount of advice Aunt Clara could give would help that particular situation.

Eva opened the blue velvet bag where she'd stored the rose quartz. Her turn had arrived to use it, and she wasn't certain she wanted to. There were certain ramifications that came with the gift the rose quartz gave that Eva didn't want to have befall her. Was finding love worth the hardships that may happen as a result? Hadn't she already endured enough. Why did love have to be difficult, too?

If she used the rose quartz to find love, then another obstacle would be put in her path. There was always a chance she would find love only to lose it. That could mean anything from the one she loved dying, or being separated from her by another means. If the latter were to happen there was always a chance they'd find each other again, but at what cost? None of it sounded like a path she wished to take. In her estimation, the rose quartz was more of a curse than a gift. She should just send it on to her cousin. Eva had no intention of actually using it, and as it was a family heirloom, she didn't wish to lose it either.

Carefully, Eva placed the rose quartz back inside the velvet bag and pulled the strings to close it tight, then put the bag inside the drawer on her writing desk. It would be safe there. She refused to place the necklace around her neck. Eva was too afraid to invoke the supposed magical properties it contained—and fear had never been a close friend of hers... She wanted freedom from her current circumstances, but at what cost? What would the rose quartz expect of her in return for granting her a chance with her one true love? She had too many questions and no clear answers. Eva hated uncertainty more than anything.

No, she couldn't do it—even if it meant she would never find love…

She would not risk something happening to the one person meant for her. Fate was fickle, and she would not tempt it to a disastrous end. She'd take her chances with whatever her lot in life turned out to be without the aid of the rose quartz. After a time, she'd send it on to her cousin, the final one of four of them, to allow her a turn. If she waited a short time none of her cousins would question her closely about her use of it. Forwarding it to her cousin too soon would make them all pester her. She had to at least pretend she was interested in the rose quartz for now. Eva had no desire to give her cousins a reason to question her or her motives. They all seemed fine with using the quartz to find love, and if she expressed any disinterest, she feared how they might react. This was what was best for her, and she didn't want to explain herself to anyone. She hated all kinds of confrontation, no matter how well meaning it could be.

A knock echoed through the chamber, causing Eva to jump. She turned toward the door. Who could be on the other side? She prayed it wasn't her aunt. Eva had been in residence at the castle for less than a sennight and already her aunt was driving her mad. Another knock. "Miss Payne," a woman said from the other side of the door. "Lady Andover wishes for you to join her in the blue salon."

Eva groaned. She was probably preparing more lessons for Eva. So far none of her lessons had made much sense. Truthfully, they were nothing more than her aunt regaling her with tales of her own season and the joys of her youth. Eva had been polite, of course, but she had been battling ennui the entire time. "Please tell her I'll join her posthaste." She kept her tone light and happy sounding and somehow managed not to stutter once. Eva did not need the maid to report her lack of enthusiasm to Aunt Clara.

She sighed and then took a deep, fortifying breath. When she faced her aunt, she would need whatever strength she could muster. Satisfied she was duly prepared for the upcoming encounter with her aunt, she smoothed her skirts one last time, then exited her chamber. Eva slowly descended the stairs. Ladies, as her aunt had said often since she'd arrived, did not run or rush to be anywhere. It would be foolish to start the encounter with a lecture on her hurried arrival.

Once she stepped inside the parlor, she waited by the entrance for her aunt to acknowledge her. Aunt Clara had a fair complexion not marred by any time spent outdoor. Her hair was dark, almost as dark as the night sky, but highlighted slightly by some silver streaked throughout. When she turned toward Eva, her blue eyes made her shiver slightly from the coldness of their depths.

"Evangeline," her aunt greeted her. "Come forward, girl, and sit. I don't want to look up at you the entire time."

Eva swallowed the lump in her throat and did as

her aunt asked. She sat in the chair directly across from her aunt. When she had first arrived, she had deigned to sit closer and had come to regret that decision. It was far easier for her aunt to reach out and smack her with her cane if she was within reach. "The maid told me you required me to attend to you." Eva struggled not to stutter. She was afraid of Aunt Clara, but if she couldn't keep from stumbling over the words, her aunt would find some way to punish her for it. The few days she'd spent in her company had been harsh ones, and forced her to speak very carefully. She never let words spill off her tongue without first thinking about what she should say and then deliberately pronouncing each one.

"Yes," her aunt agreed. "I did send for you. There are a few things we need to discuss."

That did not bode well for Eva… "About?" She lifted a brow. Eva probably should refrain from being impertinent, but this was something she had to know.

"Your future, of course," her aunt clarified. "I see no reason why you have not secured a match yet. You come from a solid family line and you are passably pretty."

Such kind words her aunt had for her… Eva

barely managed to suppress the urge to roll her eyes. Besides, her aunt *was* right. She did come from an excellent family and her blonde hair and blue eyes were at least more favorable in the eyes of the ton. Those things had never been the issue. She glanced away from her aunt and tried to keep the fear from her voice, but failed. "It..s not my fam… fam…family connections." Damn it. She'd been doing so well.

"No," her aunt agreed. The disapproval in her tone was evident as she spoke. "But we can work on your…speech difficulties."

Eva turned to face her aunt. "I've bbbeen trying," she said. Shame spread through her as she spoke. Why couldn't she stop stuttering? Her cheeks heated from the frustration with her inability to speak properly.

"Not hard enough," Aunt Clara said in a firm tone. She narrowed her gaze and studied Eva. She resisted the urge to squirm under the scrutiny. Her aunt settled her hand over her cane and leaned back as if satisfied with some decision she'd made. "We are going to ensure that will no longer be a deterrent for you. Starting with a house party over Christmastide." A smugness settled over her aunt that troubled Eva.

She forced herself to calm down and articulate her words. Eva had to keep her wits about her to navigate the rest of their conversation, and stuttering would make it all inherently worse. "A house party?" She thought she would be free from social engagements until the start of the season. That had been the only blessing she could see about being sent to the remote area of Wales. "Christmastide is a mere sennight away. Is there time to arrange a proper house party?"

"I have already begun doing so." Her aunt leaned forward, pressing her cane into the carpet. "Invitations were sent before you arrived. Our first guests will start to arrive tomorrow." Her lips tilted upward into a self-satisfied smile.

How awful… Why was her aunt just now telling her this? There was no helping any of it of course. This was her life for the foreseeable future. Her aunt had complete control over her. Eva's father had ensured that when he'd exiled her to the castle. "How many guests will be here?" She had to gain as much information as possible. It would be the only ammunition available to her. She needed as much help as she could to survive the upcoming house party.

"Several gentlemen," her aunt informed her. "At

least three eligible ones. I had to invite some ladies too or it wouldn't be even numbers in attendance, and well, it would not look right. If I were you, I'd take advantage of the close proximity and lure one of those gentlemen into matrimony."

Surely her aunt wasn't suggesting she trap one of them into marriage... That couldn't be right at all. Aunt Clara was far too prudish to suggest anything so untoward. "I don't know if that is possible, but I will try to gain the attention of one of them." Even if that attention wasn't of the romantic sort. Eva had to at least try to converse with them. Her aunt wouldn't allow anything less.

"Do more than that." Her aunt's tone was firm. "I expect that after Christmastide, I can write your father of your impending nuptials." Well... It seemed as if her aunt had higher expectations than Eva had believed. Aunt Clara stared at Eva for several moments, unblinking. "Do not let me down, girl."

What else was she supposed to say to that? She *would not* trap some unsuspecting gentleman into marriage. Eva wanted more than that with a husband. She hoped to find love, or at the very least, a mutual respect. If she forced a man to marry her, surely he would come to resent her for it.

Then what kind of marriage would she have? One where her husband loathed her? No, she refused to sentence herself, and some unsuspecting gentleman, to a lifetime of misery. "I promise to do my best." She would not promise to do anything she found appalling.

"That's what I'm afraid of." Her aunt sighed. "But don't you worry, girl, I'm here, and I will not allow you to fail."

And that was what Eva feared after hearing what her aunt had to say... If Eva couldn't force a marriage to happen, her aunt would. This upcoming house party would be a social disaster. If she didn't find a husband, she might very well end up ruined at the end of it.

She took a breath to calm herself. "I'm certain that will make my father happy." Eva didn't believe her father cared what happened to her as long as he was no longer responsible for her care. She was not a male child and therefore he had little use for her. He'd married not long ago and was doing his best to impregnate his new bride with his heir. Eva was not important, and never had been.

"Of course he will be. That is why he sent you to me, after all." Aunt Clara lifted her chin. There was a haughtiness in her gaze that was foreboding.

"I have also had the maids go through your gowns. Most will be fine for the house party but you did not bring any ballgowns. A seamstress will be here in the morning to take your measurements. You will be dressed appropriately for the Christmas ball. That is when I hope to announce your betrothal."

Her aunt was overconfident about her chances of securing a match at this house party. What would she do when Eva undoubtedly failed? She wanted to run and hide, but that would not solve her problem. It was time to put her head high and quit being the timid mouse she'd been for years. "All right," she said in a soft tone. "Is there anything else?" She hoped not...

"No," Aunt Clara said. "Go rest. It will be the last time you can for a while. Tomorrow is the start of your new future. Prepare yourself, because nothing will ever be the same again."

She nodded. "Yes, Aunt Clara," she said, then stood and turned on her heels to leave. She forced herself to walk at a proper pace. If she rushed out of the room it would give her aunt the satisfaction of knowing she'd unnerved her. Aunt Clara had disrupted Eva's small world in ways her aunt would never understand.

Eva didn't have to wait until the next day for

her life to change. It had the moment she'd been told she would have to stay in Wales over the winter months. Nothing had been the same since her father had decreed his sister would be her tutor and help Eva find a husband. She had known then that her life would be full of constant upheaval, and the fact she'd been right did not make it better.

She went directly to her chamber, and once there plopped down on the bed and gave in to the urge to cry. Later, there would be no time for tears, and it was best to get the anguish out and only show strength afterward. If she had any chance of helping herself, she would have to find her inner strength and hold on to it with all she had inside of her. She couldn't counsel herself. All she could do was try to be reasonable and move forward as best she could.

Two

Sebastian Gray, the Earl of Somerset, tapped his fingers impatiently against the arm of his chair. He had been summoned to the home office by his uncle, the Duke of Wharton, and no one ignored a command from the duke. Not even his favorite nephew… Bas had been doing his uncle's bidding for as long as he could remember. Wharton had been more of a father to him than his own had been. Not that the former earl had been alive long enough to be a father to begin with. Bas's father had been a wastrel and died how he lived… with a bottle of good whiskey and a whore by his side. No one really knew what happened, but that didn't make him any less dead.

Bas's mother had been devastated. Not because

there was any true love between her and the dead earl, but because of the scandal that had followed. She couldn't handle all the loud whispers and sly glances in her direction. A fortnight after Bas's father's death, his mother fled the country. She went on an extended tour of the continent, and never returned. Bas had been left in the Duke of Wharton's care and he didn't spare his mother a second thought. She hadn't done so for him, so why should he bother with her? He doubted he would recognize her if they ever crossed paths. It had been that long since he'd last gazed upon her, and frankly, he hoped she never grazed him with her presence ever again. He had no need for a woman that didn't bother to care for her own child.

"Hello, Bas," his uncle greeted him. The Duke of Wharton sat behind his large oak desk and leaned back in his chair. "You look well." His uncle's hair was dark and streaked with gray at the sides. His light blue eyes were cold, almost ice like in appearance, but they warmed up when he was truly happy—a rare occurrence, but it happened at times.

"I am," he agreed. This was not necessarily an unusual start to their conversation, but there was something odd in the duke's expression. Bas couldn't quite discern what was different, but it left him unsettled. "You wished to see me."

"I did," the duke replied, but didn't immediately elaborate. The silence in the room was almost deafening. Bas didn't like it and fought the urge to fill the void with inane conversation. He knew better than to babble like an idiot in his uncle's presence though. The duke didn't suffer fools, and while Bas played one at times, he had never been as unintelligent as many believed him to be.

Bas started to fidget in his seat—he wasn't perfect after all. What was going on in that diabolical mind of the duke's? He had a feeling when the duke finally spoke, he wouldn't like one word of it. Still, Bas knew from experience he couldn't rush the duke into saying a word before he was ready to. He would explain everything in his own way, and in his own time. Nothing would or could make the duke do anything he didn't wish to. "I need you to do me a favor," his uncle finally said.

Somehow, Bas held in the groan that had formed at the back of his throat. His uncle's idea of a favor always turned out terribly for Bas. The last favor had Bas acting the fool in polite society, so anyone and everyone believed him a complete ninny—and he'd never lived down that assumption.

Much to his uncle's delight, and Bas was forced to pretend to be that affable idiot ever since. He lifted a brow. "What exactly is this favor?" One Bas would not be able to refuse—he'd never been able to say no to the duke.

"It's more than one, actually." The duke frowned. Bas held back a sigh. This was not going to be good… "Seraphina and Agatha have been invited to a house party."

His cousin, Seraphina, was popular in the ton. She was the daughter of a duke and had a dowry that fortune hunters drooled over. That made his uncle extra protective of her. Agatha was Wharton's ward. He'd taken her in when her father, Baron Cartwright, had died. Agatha had been two, and an orphan since her mother died at her birth. Much like Bas, Agatha had never truly known either of her parents.

Bas sighed. "Please tell me you don't wish for me to attend with them."

The duke just stared at him. Bas's heart flipped and his stomach plummeted. He did not wish to attend any house party. They were never fun for him. "It's more than that," the duke began. "Yes, I do need you to escort them." He ran his hand through his dark hair. "But only because it will be a good cover for what I really need."

And it only got worse… "You need me to continue to act the fool."

There was only one reason his uncle ever wanted him to attend a social function. Bas was his inside man. Because they all thought him an unintelligent addle pate, they said things in front of him they would never do otherwise. It made him the duke's perfect spy. He couldn't wait until the day he could no longer pretend to be oblivious.

"I do." He leaned forward. "There is a smuggling ring that operates near the coast of Wales, in the area of St. Davids. The town is short distance from the Seabury Castle where the house party is located, and it is situated along a cove that is perfect for a smuggling if one has the inclination—and someone does."

"What makes you think the smugglers work near this castle?" His uncle always had excellent information and if he thought there were smugglers, there would be smugglers, but Bas had to have all the details if he was to be the spy the duke needed.

"I have someone working near the town. He will make contact with you once you arrive, but I need solid proof if we are going to make any moves. This involves, or possibly does, a member of the aristocracy. I can't do anything unless there is irrefutable evidence."

Bas cursed under his breath. This got worse and worse… A member of the aristocracy could make his life miserable. In fact, he probably should count on it. Still, he couldn't say no. "When do we leave?"

His uncle smiled and stood. He walked over to his decanter of brandy and poured two glasses, then handed one to Bas. "At dawn," he told him, then sipped his brandy. "Seraphina and Agatha are already preparing for the journey. Have your trunk delivered to Wharton house and stay in your old room. It will make leaving easier in the morning."

As usual, the duke was right. He hated losing even a small amount of his independence, though. Bas had yet to set up residence at Somerset Manor or his own townhouse in London. He'd chosen to take a bachelor apartment since he was rarely in town. His uncle kept sending him off on missions of some sort. "I'll do this on one condition." He had to set down some sort of rules or his uncle would keep having him do his spying. "That after this, I am free. I'm tired and I want to start being the earl and restore my family name."

The duke waved his hand. "That's not necessary and you know it. One day you'll have my title and it is all the prestige you'll need."

Bas just stared at him. "That is a long way off, and I want to be my own man. I'm done being a fool for you."

His uncle smiled. "All right. How about we make a compromise, then?"

He didn't want to compromise, but perhaps he should hear what his uncle had to say. "What's your offer?"

"When you marry, I'll stop asking you to spy for me," he said, then grinned. As if this was something he thought Bas would never agree to. His uncle was wrong. He'd gladly find a wife if it allowed him a different kind of freedom. "Until then, you will work for me as I need it."

"All right," Bas agreed, then downed the contents of his glass. He let the burn from the brandy fill his throat and he felt good after. This was exactly what he needed. "I can agree with that. Now if you'll excuse me, I am going to go pack. I have a house party to prepare for."

Bas didn't give his uncle a chance to reply. He stood and left the duke's office and didn't look back once.

Bas sat up on the bed and groaned. He hadn't been able to sleep much the night before. This trip to the remote area of Wales was not something he looked forward to. It was going to be so much worse with Seraphina and Agatha along. Seraphina more than Agatha… He loved his younger cousin, but she was a shrew at times. Especially when she didn't get her way. Her red hair was the only outer indication of her fiery nature. Agatha was far more demure and steady. She didn't make noise and was too obedient. She should be a little more like Seraphina, but she couldn't seem to be less strict with her demeanor. Perhaps this house party would help her relax a little. Bas hoped so anyway.

He dressed quickly and went down to the dining room. Cook would have risen early enough to make them a hearty meal before their excursion, and if Bas knew the cook, he expected a basket of food for the journey as well. He adored Mrs. Harrow and had often visited with her in the kitchen as a boy. She made the best biscuits and tarts. He hoped she packed several of those in the basket of food. In fact, Mrs. Harrow's treats were the only ones he ever enjoyed. Any others didn't compare and he never liked eating them.

When he entered the dining room, he found Agatha already seated at the table. She was nibbling on a piece of toast. There was tea on the table, but she had no other food on her plate. "You need to eat more than toast," he told her. "It's going to be a long and tedious journey."

She frowned. Her dark hair was pulled up into a simple chignon and her green eyes held no humor in them. "I cannot eat anything heavy in the morning. When I do I get ill."

He did recall that she hadn't seemed to have much on her plate for the morning meal in the past. How had he forgotten that? They would need a basket of food from Mrs. Harrow more than ever now. Seraphina might skip breakfast as well. Though her reasons would not be the same as Agatha's. Seraphina tended to worry she would gain too much weight and often skipped meals to keep her figure trim. Instead of addressing Agatha's lack of food, Bas asked, "Are you excited about this house party?"

"Are you?" she quipped.

He grinned. "Well, at least we can depend upon each other for entertainment."

Agatha wrinkled her nose. "Are you going to act like you don't have a thought inside your brain while we are there?"

He sighed, then nodded. "I promised the duke I would."

"I wish he would let you stop doing that." She lifted her tea and sipped it. "I find it rather annoying to go along with your charade. I hate lies."

He couldn't blame her for that outlook. "I'm not particularly fond of them myself." Bas sat at the table and not long after, a footman brought out a plate of food for him. His plate was full of eggs, kippers, and sausage. He lifted the teapot and filled his cup. "But hopefully I won't have to pretend for much longer. This trip may be the last time."

"The last time for what?" Seraphina asked as she entered the dining room. She sat next to Agatha with a flourish. Trust Seraphina to make an entrance even when there was only family around. Her bright red hair was pinned up in a far more elaborate style than Agatha's. There were so many braids and twists Bas didn't even want to begin figuring out how her maid had wound it all together.

"Bas has to pretend to be addle pated again," Agatha said, then took a bite of her toast.

Seraphina turned her attention to him. "That's unfortunate for you. I don't understand how you can act like a ninny so often. Anyone with a brain has to see there is intelligence in your eyes."

"You only say that because you have known me your entire life." Bas shrugged. "Besides the individuals that matter know the truth." His closest friends understood what he did for the duke. When he was in school, he struggled with his education. It took him longer to learn how to read because he kept mixing up the letters. The other boys had made fun of him and his reputation as being unintelligent had grown from there. Caleb, the Duke of Riverdale, and Roarke, the Marquess of Huntington, had helped him overcome his difficulties. They had shared a room with him at Eton when he'd attended. When it was time for him to continue his education, Bas had hired tutors instead of going to Oxford. The embarrassment had been too much for him, and he could learn at a slower pace with tutors. He still had an excellent education. His uncle had ensured it.

"Still," Seraphina began. "How are you to find a wife when they all think you are empty-headed?"

She shook her head. "You're going to end up with a simpleton for a bride."

Bas hoped not, but at least he'd be free from his obligations to the duke if he had a wife—for that even a simpleton would suffice. "I'll worry about that when I start searching for a wife. I won't be doing anything of the sort during this house party." He grinned. "Are you husband hunting?"

Seraphina shrugged. "I'm not certain what I expect from this house party. If I find a husband, then I'll be free to enjoy the season this spring. If I don't, then I'll still enjoy it. I'm in no rush to tie myself down."

Bas nodded. "A wise decision." He turned toward Agatha. "What do you want from this house party?"

She met his gaze. "To be left alone. I have no desire to marry anyone. I'll most likely look for a position as a governess or a lady's companion. I don't want a family or a man to depend on for my fortune."

Agatha had a plan, at least. Though Bas suspected her view had more to do with her orphan status than she would ever admit. A family meant obligations and the possibility of loss. Agatha had lost far too much already in her life. Bas understood her reluctance to let anyone in and risk losing them, too.

"Well," he began. "Either way, we're going to be together through it all." Bas pushed his plate away. "I'll meet you two in the carriage." With those words, he left Seraphina and Agatha to their meal. He'd lost his appetite and wished he could find a way to avoid the upcoming house party. Something told him that this trip, this party, would change his life forever, and he wasn't certain how he felt about that possibility.

Three

This house party is a terrible idea. Eva kept repeating that inside her head over and over again, but it changed nothing. She would still have to endure it and socialize with her aunt's guests. The guests that had already arrived were not...pleasant. Lady Hazel Williams, the Countess of Dowden, was a horrible person and her daughter, Lady Jane Williams, mimicked her mother's personality. Lady Dowden was one of her Aunt Clara's closest friends. She could have gone her whole life without having the privilege of being introduced to the countess. Her aunt's dearest friend was the worst sort of person...judgmental, snobbish, and cruel.

"When will the rest of the guests arrive?" Lady Dowden asked.

"Any day now," Aunt Clara answered. "Everyone has accepted the invitation. We're quite remote so the travel time for everyone will be great. Thankfully, the weather has been favorable."

Eva almost snorted. It was bitterly cold, but she supposed her aunt was right in one regard. It hadn't snowed in several days, so at least there appeared to be a clear path for her guests. Though if she were to judge the guests that were yet to arrive by Lady Dowden and Lady Jane, Eva hoped that an enormous snowstorm would delay their arrival.

"It has been a mild winter so far," Lady Jane replied.

Eva wanted to roll her eyes. Lady Jane was quite the conversationalist. *And sarcasm, even internally, wasn't going to add anything either...* She never added anything of interest and mostly agreed with her mother and Eva's aunt. Lady Jane had no opinion of her own, and the few times Eva had been alone with her, she'd been spiteful and callous.

"Do you think the weather will remain pleasant?" Eva couldn't help herself. She had to add to their tedious conversation. If they were going to pretend there was nothing of interest to discuss, then she had no reason to prevent that. Besides, she would rather they didn't turn their maliciousness toward her.

"I don't see any reason it won't," her aunt supplied. "For your sake, I hope at least all the gentlemen manage to arrive."

And that right there was a reason to keep her mouth closed and her opinions to herself. Once they realized she was still in the room, she became a handy target for their barbed tongues. So far she had kept her stutter to a minimum, but both Lady Dowden and her daughter had noticed it. Their opinion had been hateful, of course. Why did her aunt like these two women? Eva shook that thought away. She understood it quite well, but she didn't like it. Her aunt was of their ilk, and together they made it easier for them to be hateful.

"I don't mind not finding a husband," Eva said. "But since you and my father deem it of utmost importance, I will do my best to find a gentleman willing to marry me posthaste."

"I wish you luck," Lady Jane said, then snorted. She turned her attention to Aunt Clara and asked, "What gentlemen did you invite?"

"The Duke of Riverdale, the Marquess of Huntington, the Earl of Moray, The Duke of Wharton," she said, then tapped her chin. "Though the Duke of Wharton probably won't be in the market for a wife, even though he is a widower. Rumor has it he's content to let his title go to that half-wit nephew of his."

"The Earl of Somerset?" Lady Dowden asked. She wrinkled her nose in distaste. "He's a handsome gentleman at least, even if he doesn't have an intelligent thought inside his head."

"He's definitely gorgeous," Lady Jane agreed.

Eva had never met the Earl of Somerset, and she already felt pity for him. These ladies had reduced him to nothing but something pretty to look upon. The poor man… "What does he look like?" She couldn't stop the words from spilling from her mouth. She regretted them immediately.

"Why?" Lady Jane asked and raised her eyebrow. "Do you think because he's a fool, you can trick him into marriage?" She laughed as if she'd said something hilarious. Eva felt as if she'd suffered a blow directly to her stomach.

"No," Eva said carefully. "I'm curious what it is about him you find appealing despite his lack of intelligence." If the Earl of Somerset attended the house party, Eva would have to make it her mission to befriend him. No one deserved to be the brunt of such deliberate cruelty.

"I'll tell you," Lady Jane said. "So you can seek him out if you're ever at the same social gathering." She sneered. "You do need all the assistance you can get. He's tall, and has thick black hair that makes you want to run your fingers through it, and his eyes…" She sighed dreamily. "They're as green as grass on a warm summer day. He has such warmth in those eyes you almost forget how stupid he is."

The way Lady Jane spoke about Lord Somerset made Eva think she'd happily marry him if he asked. "You haven't set your cap for him, then?"

Lady Jane glared at her. "There's no guarantee his uncle won't marry again and produce an heir. I would much rather set my sights on the Duke of Riverdale. That title is firmly set, and he's also quite handsome."

The Duke of Riverdale was unlikely to give Lady Jane a second glance. Eva had been introduced to the duke. He was quite handsome, too. His golden hair was appealing, but his eyes were cold. They were ice blue and could freeze someone with one glance. The hardness that he showed the world had made Eva keep her distance. He also didn't seem the type to suffer fools or mean-spirited people. Lady Jane wouldn't secure that particular match. Eva would bet her entire inheritance, small though it was, on that.

"Pardon me, Lady Andover," the butler, Mr. Pennyworth, said from the entrance of the sitting room. "Some guests have arrived."

Lady Jane clapped her hands. "How exciting."

"I'll be there momentarily to greet them," Aunt Clara told Mr. Pennyworth. "Have the housekeeper ensure their rooms are prepared, and one of the maids show them where to find them. Also have the cook prepare more tea and biscuits for refreshments."

"Yes, my lady," Pennyworth said. Then he turned on his heels to leave.

Her aunt rose to her feet. "Evangeline, please come with me. I expect you to act as hostess when I am unavailable." She turned toward Lady Dowden and Lady Jane. "We shouldn't be long. If the tea arrives before we join you again, feel free to pour for yourselves." She turned toward Eva and gestured for her to follow. Eva took a deep breath and did her best to calm herself. This was a test, and she prayed she passed it.

THE JOURNEY TO THIS REMOTE CASTLE HAD BEEN AS tedious as Bas had expected it to be. The trip had taken an entire sennight, and Seraphina had complained the entire time. At least Agatha had kept her opinion to herself, though it was clear to him she'd been equally as uncomfortable. When they had finally arrived at Seabury Castle, he had breathed a sigh of relief. At least until he remembered he would have to act like an idiot once he was inside the bloody castle.

"Lady Andover will be with you shortly. I'll have a footman take your trunks to your assigned bedchambers." The butler told them. "Mrs. Simmons will show you to your rooms after Lady Andover has greeted you. Refreshments can be found in the blue salon if you wish to join the countess and the guests that have already arrived in a half hour."

Bas stared past the butler and frowned. Did the countess expect them to join her so soon after their arrival? Seraphina and Agatha would probably wish to rest immediately. He couldn't wait until his duties were done with and he could return home. Of course, he'd have to find a wife to be completely free from his obligations, but that was a worry for another day. "Did you say Lady Andover would be unable to greet us?" He asked in an absentminded tone.

"No…" the butler started to say but was interrupted.

"I would never be so rude," a woman said as she strolled into the foyer. She had dark hair streaked with silver, but that wasn't what made Bas stand up straighter. There was a bit of cruelty in her features. Her blue eyes were hard and held a hint of anger in them. What had made this woman so angry? "This is my niece, Miss Evangeline Payne."

Her niece was the exact opposite of her. She had golden blonde hair and light blue eyes. They reminded him of a bright summer sky and filled him with warmth. She glanced downward, not meeting his gaze or looking toward Seraphina or Agatha.

"It's a pleasure to meet you," Seraphina said. "This is Miss Agatha Cartwright, my father's, the Duke of Wharton's ward." She gestured toward

Agatha, who stared at Lady Andover as if she'd grown an extra head. Agatha didn't like their hostess. "My father could not attend. Luckily, my cousin, Lord Somerset, was available." She beamed at Bas. "He's a dear man for giving up his holiday plans so Agatha and I could attend."

Bas kept sneaking glances at Lady Andover's niece. He wanted to learn more about her, but she didn't appear to want to be there. "It was nothing," Bas said dismissively. "Did someone say we would have something to eat?" He rubbed his stomach. "I'm starving. When is our next meal?"

He wasn't that hungry, but it was part of his act. Bas would much rather retire to his chamber for several moments of blissful peace. He couldn't do that yet, though. He had to establish his persona and find out what he could.

"We will have an enjoyable meal this evening." Lady Andover glared at him. "Tea and biscuits will have to suffice for the moment."

"What kind of biscuits?" He stared around the foyer as if looking for the tasty treats. Bas was actually taking note of his surroundings. It was best to be prepared for any possibility. "I like lemon ones." He actually hated most biscuits. Sweet treats were not favorites of his unless they were made by the

Duke of Wharton's cook. She was a genius in the kitchen. He'd much rather have some bread and cheese. That would be far more filling. "Or maybe some dusted with sugar?" He rubbed his stomach. "I'm ever so hungry."

Lady Andover rolled her eyes. "I'm certain cook has made some spectacular biscuits."

The housekeeper joined them. "I can show you to your quarters now if you'll follow me."

Bas waved his hand. "I can find it later. I'm more interested in these biscuits Lady Andover has been raving about." He turned toward the countess. "Show me where to find them."

"Well…I…" Lady Andover sputtered. "A maid will bring them into the salon when they're ready."

"I can't eat them yet?" He frowned. "Then why did you say I could?"

"I didn't…"

He sighed. "I suppose I can go find the kitchen myself. It's such an inconvenience."

Miss Evangeline Payne giggled. He turned toward her and stared. His curiosity about her was growing the more time he spent with her—short that it'd been so far, it'd been enough to intrigue him. Why was she so quiet?

"I can't allow you to do that," Lady Andover

said in a snobbish tone. "That's most inappropriate." So his host was a stickler for societal rules. That was helpful information.

"But Aunt Clara," Miss Evangeline said in a pleading tone. "He is hungry, and they have traveled quite a distance to attend the house party. Should we not offer him more refreshments?"

She glared at her niece. "He can wait a few moments longer. I doubt he'll perish before then."

"Agatha and I are going to our chambers," Seraphina glared at Bas. "Enjoy your biscuits." His cousin had already grown irritated with his foolish persona…

Bas had to hold in the laugh threatening to spill from inside of him. Seraphina knew he disliked most biscuits, and wouldn't actually eat many if he could help it. She was probably secretly hoping he would be forced to eat the entire lot of them. "I'll see you at the evening meal," he yelled after them. Then he turned toward the countess and her niece. "Now please lead the way. I do need to inspect those biscuits to make sure they're edible. Otherwise, I will have to insist on something more substantial. I might die if I don't get some food."

Over-dramatization was his friend and he would use it to his advantage. The countess rolled her eyes, but she tried to hide it. Miss Evangeline Payne seemed to come alive a little, though. Her eyes sparkled with amusement she couldn't contain. He would have to find a moment alone with her and uncover all her secrets. Until then, he had his part to play…

Four

Dinner had been terrible. Not that Eva had expected much from it. She couldn't wait to escape to her bedchamber for the night, but there was no way Aunt Clara would allow her to leave the parlor yet. All the ladies had agreed to retire there after dinner. With Lord Somerset being the only gentleman in attendance, he could either join them or retire for the evening. She wished she had gotten the latter choice.

She sighed.

Lord Somerset was so lucky he'd been born male. Even if the ladies all seemed to believe him empty headed. Eva suspected that wasn't entirely accurate. There was something about him that didn't quite seem right. She didn't know what, but she was determined to uncover his secret. Maybe she would find him alone while he attended this house party and ask him a few questions. Eva wanted to know more about him. Perhaps if she tried to be friendly with his cousin Lady Seraphina Bell or his uncle's ward, Miss Agatha Cartwright—then she might be more likely to have the opportunity to converse with him. Those two ladies didn't seem as horrid as Lady Jane.

"How was your journey to Seabury Castle?" Lady Jane asked Miss Agatha and Lady Seraphina.

Miss Agatha didn't even acknowledge Lady Jane. She stood and wandered over to a nearby window and stared outside with a hopeful expression. What was she hoping she'd see out there? If she prayed for a snowstorm to save her, it was a little late for that. Lady Seraphina stared at Miss Agatha and then shook her head. She turned her attention to Lady Jane. "It wasn't pleasant." She didn't elaborate, but her tone said a lot. It was cold and unrelenting—as if conversing with Lady Jane were a chore she abhorred.

Lady Jane was not accustomed to being dismissed, and even though it was horrid—Eva was secretly pleased. Especially since it was the daughter of a duke giving her so little attention. Lady Jane opened and closed her mouth several times. Then began speaking, "Did you hear that the Duke of Riverdale and the Marquess of Huntington are going to attend the house party?"

"Are they?" Lady Seraphina yawned. "How unusual for them. They must be experiencing a fit of ennui." Clearly, Lady Seraphina was a bit apathetic toward her surroundings as well.

Eva had to agree with her. She wanted to go home, or at least visit her grandmother. She lived along the Irish Sea and it wasn't more than a half day's journey to her estate. If only her father would let her stay there instead… It wasn't any more entertaining there than with Aunt Clara, but at least she was more welcome there. "Perhaps we should play a game." It might help to pass the time they were forced to spend together, anyway. It was also a chance to form some sort of rapport with the two ladies she preferred to Lady Jane.

"I'd rather not," Lady Seraphina replied. "I'm still exhausted from the carriage ride. Traveling doesn't agree with me." She smiled at Eva. "Perhaps tomorrow evening. What sort of games do you enjoy?" At least she hadn't been dismissive of her as she had Lady Jane. She hadn't bothered to smile at the other woman.

"I don't have a preference," she answered. "I'm willing to try any you suggest." Eva hadn't found any parlor games she enjoyed. They were all tedious and required more than she wanted to do.

"Then we can decide tomorrow. Perhaps we can play a hand of whist." She turned her attention to Miss Agatha. "Will you play with us, Agatha?"

Miss Agatha turned around and nodded. "If you insist." She then glanced at Lady Jane. "Did you say the Duke of Riverdale was coming here?"

"I did," Lady Jane answered in an energetic tone. She was probably happy someone was as interested as she was in the duke's attendance.

"How odd," Miss Agatha replied. "It really is unlike him or Lord Huntington to attend parties. At least not ones that involve ladies." She frowned. "I wonder what they're up to."

Lady Jane glared at her. "I expect they're hoping to be entertained."

"I doubt that very much." Miss Agatha said dismissively. "They are capable of entertaining themselves without bothering to travel to some-where as remote as Seabury Castle."

It appeared as if Lady Seraphina and Miss

Agatha were well acquainted with the duke and the marquess. "Why do you believe they're coming?" Eva asked Miss Agatha. "Since you're acquainted with them."

Lady Seraphina waved her hand. "They're closer to Bas—I mean Lord Somerset— than us. We're forced to spend time with them when they visit Wharton Manor or are in town. They all went to Eton together."

That was interesting, Eva thought. Perhaps they were only attending to spend time with the Earl of Somerset. He was Bas to his close friends and family it seemed. Eva liked that nickname. It suited the earl from the little she knew of him. She wanted to ask them more questions about Lord Somerset, but held back. Any interest she showed a gentleman would be noted by her aunt, who thankfully had paid little attention to their conversation. She seemed lost in conversation with Lady Dowden. "Do you ever wish you could have gone away to school?"

"Ladies," Lady Jane drew out the word, distain dripping from her voice. "Do not *study*," she finished in a cool tone. "We do not need to fill our heads with useless information."

"How do you know it isn't useful?" Lady

Seraphina lifted a brow. "If you never bothered to learn."

"Considering your cousin went to Eton and is known to be stupid, I think that's all the answer I need." Lady Jane tilted her chin into the air. Her snobbishness was rearing its ugly head.

Lady Seraphina sneered at her. "Your ignorance is shining brightly, my dear. Be careful what assumptions you make about the people in your current sphere. You never know when you may have made a grave error and your social acceptance is about to be eradicated." With those words, Lady Seraphina stood. "Agatha, I'm going to retire. Would you like to join me?"

"Oh, yes," Miss Agatha said. "The company here is leaving an unpleasant taste in my mouth." She turned toward Eva. "Not you. I don't find any fault so far with your behavior. I do hope that doesn't change."

Eva put a hand over her mouth and coughed to stop the laughter from spilling out. "I don't plan on being rude in the future," she replied after she lowered her hand. "Have a good rest."

"Until tomorrow," Lady Seraphina said. She didn't look in Lady Jane's direction. Eva liked these two ladies a great deal. She had a feeling they would be good friends.

Bas had never been so grateful to be the only gentleman for miles. Apparently, Lord Andover was in the next town over for some sort of meeting and wouldn't return until morning. That was highly suspicious, and the reason the Duke of Wharton had sent him to this cold, vile castle. He intensely disliked Lady Andover, Lady Dowden, and Lady Jane. He was reserving judgement on Miss Evangeline. She wasn't so easy to read. Though he did believe her to be much kinder than the other three.

He felt a bit ashamed to have abandoned Seraphina and Agatha, but they would understand. None of them were there for the company. When the duke gave an order, he expected it to be followed, and no one dared to question him. They had all learned that lesson at an early age. With the Earl of Andover not in residence, it would be much easier to search his study and personal space. Though he would still have to be careful. There were still servants lurking around and other people inside Seabury that might question him if he were to be caught.

He had already sneaked into the earl's chambers and searched. Bas had found nothing of interest there, but that had probably been his only chance to go in and look around. He would do the study and library, then retire for the evening. He might not be able to do much more searching that night. It would be highly suspect if he were caught in the middle of the night. Perhaps he should save the study for another day and go to the library first. At least he could use the excuse of looking for something to read if he were interrupted in there.

With that decision made, he strolled down the corridor to head toward the library. One of the footman had shown him around earlier that day. After the debacle involving the biscuits, which had been as awful as he had feared—they were dry and tasteless. Somehow, he had managed to eat them all, though. Much to Lady Andover's horror... The expression on her face had been worth stomaching those horrid biscuits.

When he reached the library, he set down the candelabra he'd been carrying. He debated lighting some more candles, so it would be easier to look around without having to carry the candleholders.

Instead, he lifted it and set it on the desk and started to look through the drawers. He found a ledger and started to flip through it. The sound of feet shuffling on the floor outside the library had him shoving it inside the drawer and closing it shut. He could look at it again later.

Bas turned toward a nearby shelf and peeked at the contents. Books on farming…how quaint and boring.

"Lord Somerset," a woman said from behind him. He turned around and met Miss Evangeline's gaze. He tilted his lips upward into a smile. This was a development he liked. He had been hoping to spend some time with her alone. She was an enigma he hoped to solve.

"Miss Evangeline," he greeted, then bowed. "You look lovely in candlelight.

"I…I…" She swallowed hard, then spoke again. Miss Evangeline jutted her chip upward in defiance. He appreciated a woman who could speak up for herself. "You don't need to charm me."

He lifted a brow. "Because you're incapable of being charmed?"

She shook her head. "Not at all," she blurted out. "It's just…unnecessary."

He frowned. Bas wanted to push her to give him

a better answer, but didn't think it was the right time to do so. "What brings you here?" he asked instead.

She tilted her head to the side. "Why does one usually visit a library?"

"I wouldn't know," he said in a simple tone. He still had to play the dimwit with her. "Why do they?" Bas tilted his head to the side as if her were pondering the question.

Lady Evangeline shook her head and laughed. "Well, generally it is to find a book to read."

"Oh, yes," he agreed. "That's why I came in here." He turned toward the shelf. "I need something that is going to help me fall asleep."

She walked over to his side and peered at the shelf. "I would have to agree with your choice, then." Miss Evangeline wrinkled her nose, and he found it utterly breathtaking. He wanted to lean down and press his lips to hers and discover what she might do. Would she return the kiss? "Books on farming should help you sleep for weeks, I'd think."

"What?" he said and blinked several times. He felt like the dolt he was supposed to be. What had they been discussing?

"The books silly," she said. "On farming." Miss

Evangeline pointed to them. "Or would you like something else to read?"

"Honestly, I find any books distressing." That was the truth, really. He had to really concentrate to read, so he only tried with books that mattered. Farming was not high on that list. Though he probably should learn a little if he was to take over the Somerset estate and make something of it. The duke had been managing it for him for years.

"Oh, how terrible." She met his gaze. "I adore books. Well, not all books. Some are quite tedious." She pointed to the shelf with books on farming. "Those would be terrible to read, don't you think?"

"Absolutely," he said without thinking. He would have agreed with her if she had declared the sky to be a soft shade of green, grass a brilliant purple mixed with dots of pink, and snow nothing but a figment of their imagination. Most people believed him a fool, and she was treating him as if he was worth her notice. He could love her for that alone. "What do you recommend I read?" He would read whatever she gave him even if it took him years to finish it.

"What do you usually like to read?" she asked.

"Not a thing if I can help it," he admitted. "But

I find myself curious what you enjoy reading. Pick a book out for me, please."

"I don't know…" She stared past him at the shelves. "What if you hate it?" Miss Evangeline nibbled on her bottom lip and he was once again transfixed by her. She was so damned lovely, and her heart appeared to match what he could see on the outside. Bas wanted her as he had never wanted a woman before. Of course he would meet a woman that intrigued him while on a bloody mission for his uncle.

"I promise I won't," he told her. He tilted his lips into a half smile. "It will take me a while to read, you know. I may not finish it before this house party is done. I've always struggled with words."

She frowned. "I'm so sorry. Perhaps we can compromise then."

He tilted his head to the side. He would do whatever she asked…he just hoped it wouldn't interfere with his mission. "What do you suggest?"

"Why don't we set time aside each day and I'll read it to you." When he didn't answer right away, she glanced away. "Unless you find my company unpleasant…"

"Not at all," he said softly. She'd been hurt in the past. He couldn't say when or how much, but she was uncertain about her appeal. Bas wanted her to realize how much potential she had. He understood more than most the pain of another's erroneous opinion. "I would love to spend more time with you, and reading seems innocent enough." God help him. How was he going to keep his hands and lips off this delectable woman? "When should we…read?" He didn't know what else to call it. Story time? He probably would have a difficult time concentrating.

"After we break our fast," she said. "It's the only time my aunt doesn't require me for something." She had bitterness in her tone when she spoke of Lady Andover. Miss Evangeline didn't seem to care for her aunt. That said a lot about her, too.

"That sounds perfect." He plucked a random farming book off of the shelf. "This will do for tonight." He leaned down close to her ear. "Sleep well tonight, Miss Evangeline. I look forward to listening to your story." With those words, he left her alone. If he didn't, he might end up kissing her, and that was a colossally bad idea. Though he fully intended to kiss her thoroughly before the conclusion of this house party…

Five

Eva couldn't stop thinking about the previous night in the library. She wasn't entirely sure what had happened between her and Lord Somerset. He had seemed very attentive and genuinely interested in what she had to say. He claimed to have trouble reading and she couldn't help wondering if that was the truth. With all the rumors circulating about him and his supposed lack of intelligence…it might be. Somehow she doubted it, though. The conversation she'd had with him hadn't led her to believe he was anything of the sort. Was he perpetuating a ruse of some sort? For what purpose?

She shook those thoughts away. It wasn't her place to decipher Lord Somerset's actions or reasons for why he did anything. Eva was barely acquainted with him. Though she would like the chance to learn more about him. Maybe when they next spent some time together, she would have the opportunity to discover something more informative about him. She was supposed to read one of her favorite stories to him. That would be her test. She would choose a book no gentleman would willingly choose to read.

"What are you woolgathering about?" her aunt asked. Eva glanced over to look at Aunt Clara. She leaned on her cane as she scrutinized Eva. What did she hope to uncover by staring at her so intently? Whatever it was Eva prayed she didn't actually find the answers. She did not want to be Aunt Clara's mission in life. It would be far better to escape her clutches and forge her own path. She wanted to continue to be an enigma—one no one, especially her aunt, could unravel.

"Nothing in particular," she answered in a noncommittal tone. She picked up a piece of toast and nibbled on it. Eva didn't have much of an appetite, but she was forcing herself to eat something. Her nerves were getting the better of her. After breakfast, she was supposed to meet with Lord Somerset in the library. Aunt Clara's presence didn't help what little appetite she had either. Her aunt was difficult on a good day

Her aunt narrowed her gaze. "I expect more guests will arrive today. I want you in the salon for afternoon tea to help greet anyone that arrives."

"Of course," she agreed. There wasn't any other answer Eva could give her aunt. "It would be my pleasure to help you welcome your guests." She hoped they weren't as insipid as Lady Jane and her odious mother. "Are you expecting anyone in particular?" Eva didn't much care who her aunt had invited. She only wanted to survive the house party with her reputation and emotions intact at the end.

"No, but I am hoping that the Duke of Riverdale and the Marquess of Huntington will arrive to even out the numbers. It's a pity that the Duke of Wharton couldn't attend and he sent that idiot nephew of his."

Eva didn't like how she spoke about Lord Somerset. Her aunt was making snap judgements without giving the earl a chance to prove her assumptions wrong. "He doesn't seem too terrible," she said. "He does seem to like biscuits, though." He had eaten them all and not allowed any of the ladies to have any. The earl had claimed he was too famished to share. It had to be a performance of some sort—but to what end? No one ate that many sweet treats otherwise. It was…odd. There were a lot of unusual things about the earl now that she had time to consider it.

"Do you honestly believe I might have a chance with a duke or a marquess?" Her aunt seemed to have too high of expectations for her. Why did she not invite any lesser titles? The earl's attendance made the guests seem more normal. She should be grateful the Duke of Wharton had not attended.

"Of course not." Her aunt snorted. "I invited them for Lady Jane, of course. She should have a high ranking gentleman to choose from." She sneered. "You, my dear, will be lucky to bag that simpleton."

Eva's heart sank inside her chest. Of course, her aunt thought higher of Lady Jane's prospects than hers. She was the girl with the stutter and always would be. It didn't matter that she'd worked so hard to overcome it, and she only stuttered when she was overwhelmed or anxious. "But you didn't expect him," she reminded her aunt.

"I invited the Earl of Moray for you," she explained. "He's getting on in years and his previous wife didn't provide him with an heir. He'll find you suitable."

The Earl of Moray? He was at least twice Eva's age. She had to suppress a shudder, or she'd gain a lecture from Aunt Clara. "When do you expect he will arrive?" So Eva could try to avoid him as much as possible. She would have to greet him at least, but the rest of the time, she wanted to keep her distance. Was it too much to hope he'd take a liking to Lady Jane instead?

"Perhaps today," Aunt Clara answered. "Are you excited at the prospect of him proposing?"

Eva suppressed a gag that developed inside her throat. She couldn't speak the truth. Her aunt would flay her with just a glance if she even tried. "You're anticipating he will already?" How could her aunt know the earl might ask Eva to be his wife? Surely, even an aging earl had standards he hoped to meet. What if he didn't want a stuttering countess?

"I've corresponded with him and he has indicated an interest. You'll have to be on your best behavior, but by the end of the house party, I believe you will be affianced." Her aunt beamed. She was so proud of her accomplishment. Eva was horrified. Surely this couldn't be the life she'd have. "If we must do something to encourage him toward that decision remains to be seen. But we should have good news to share with your father soon."

"We wouldn't want to disappoint my father." His happiness always came first. She often wondered what her mother had seen in him. Had she been forced into an unwanted marriage too? Had her father even cared about her mother? Eva wanted more than an arranged marriage. She wanted love, but she would settle for someone she respected and liked. Sometimes a person couldn't always have what they wanted most out of life. Eva needed to escape her father's ambitions and marriage seemed to be her only option for that.

"That's correct," her aunt said. "It's good you understand your place."

"I do," she told her aunt. If she disagreed, her life would only become more miserable. She had to find a husband without her aunt's aid. Otherwise, she would become the bride of an old man.

"Good. Now finish your breakfast. We can't have you taking ill." Of course not…a gentleman didn't want a sickly wife. He would already be settling for her stammer. Aunt Clara never said anything good or encouraging to her. If she continued to listen to her she'd end up with bigger anxiety than she already had.

After her aunt spoke, she proceeded to ignore Eva. She was all right with that. It gave her time to think and plan. Maybe her future was with the Earl of Somerset. He had seemed to take an interest in her. She would use that to her advantage if she could. When she met with him later, she would see if there was something there between them. Eva wasn't certain how to determine that and hoped the answer would come to her in the moment.

She might have to use an illness to escape the Earl of Moray if that didn't work... Her aunt didn't realize it, but her last words had given Eva that idea. She would use anything necessary to avoid an unwanted marriage. Didn't she deserve some inkling of happiness? Didn't everyone? She refused to believe she would have to suffer for the rest of her days.

BAS COULDN'T STOP THINKING ABOUT MISS Evangeline Payne. She was beautiful, kind, and intelligent. To him, she was perfection. He wanted the chance to court her properly and allow her to see the real him. Not the persona he showed the rest of the world. Bas wanted something real in his life. Yes, those that were important to him did know the truth. It wasn't the same, though. He couldn't allow anyone else in. If he did, he might ruin all of his uncle's carefully laid plans.

If only he wasn't at Seabury Castle to uncover a smuggling ring. Later that day his friends, the Duke of Riverdale and the Marquess of Huntington were to arrive. Once they were there with them, they could help him with his investigation. He had begged them to accept the invitation. Lady Andover had to be jumping for joy to secure their acceptance. Riverdale and Huntington didn't attend many social gatherings.

He wanted to be done with spying and missions. Bas was tired...exhausted really. He wanted to make the same choices his friends did. To stay home and not go to the next ball because an informant might be there waiting for him or go to his club for the enjoyment of it, not because some lord might be contemplating treason. This was not the life he would have chosen for himself, but it was the one he had. Still, he would make some changes, and soon. He couldn't pretend to be someone he wasn't any longer. It was slowly driving him mad. Bas wanted more out of his life. He wanted love and acceptance, and some days he didn't think he would ever truly have either one.

Bas stared out the glass doors in the library. In the spring it must be a gorgeous view. There were cliffs in the distance that led down to a beach, but right outside the doors was a garden. Everything was covered in snow currently, but if one used their imagination, they could envision what it might look like.

"Do you see anything interesting out there?" a female asked from behind him.

He turned and met Miss Evangeline's gaze. "Have you ever seen these gardens in the spring or summer?" He gestured toward them with a flick of his hand.

She shook her head. "I have not had the pleasure. This is my first visit here at Seabury Castle. My summers are usually reserved for visiting my grandmother."

There was a bit of whimsy in her tone that made him wonder about her grandmother. "Do you miss her?"

"I do," she said. She smiled but it was one filled with longing, maybe even a little pain. It made his heart ache. Bas resisted the urge to lift his hand and rub it away. "She's the one person I can always depend on." Miss Evangeline gestured toward the books. "Do you still wish for me to read to you?"

Bas wanted to pull her into his arms and kiss her. He didn't give into that urge though. If he did, she might slap him or never speak to him again. He could not give into his desire for her. Not without determining how she felt first and make sure she wanted him to kiss her. "I would like nothing more." If all he could do was sit and listen to her read a book, he'd take it. There wasn't anything else he could do regarding his mission until later. After his two friends arrived later that day, and Bas had a chance to meet with the Duke of Wharton's informant, he would have no time for her. He wanted to devote more hours to learning more about her, but he had his duty and it came first.

"I have considered what book I should read to you and I think I've chosen the perfect one." She went to a shelf and plucked a thin red book off the shelf. At least it wouldn't be a long story… "We can start with this and if you like it, and we finish it while we are both still here, we can pick a different one."

"All right," he agreed. "What is this book about?"

"Love and loss," she said. "Something most people wish for and some of us experience."

She walked over to the settee and sat down. "Come join me and we can begin."

Bas frowned. What kind of story was this, anyway? Love and loss? That didn't seem appealing at all. He went to the settee and joined her. He had agreed to this, and she was there. Bas could not be rude about it now. She had chosen one of her favorite books, and he would try his best to listen. Perhaps he might even enjoy it too.

"Now, let's begin." She flipped open the little red book and stopped at the first page. "It was late Autumn and there was a chill in the air. The leaves had turned colors, and most had already fell from the trees and scattered across the ground in waves of red, gold, and orange. None of that mattered to Lady Athena Knight. No, she had much more distressing thoughts rolling inside of her head. She currently sat in the back of the church located on her father's estate. She had picked her location in the hope that no one would notice her."

Miss Evangeline paused momentarily to take a breath before continuing to read. "She had dressed in her simplest gown of pale blue silk that matched the color of her eyes, and had her hairdresser twist her golden-brown hair into a simple knot at her nape. If she could have avoided this wedding, she would have, but that wasn't her fate. No, she would be forced to watch the man she loved marry someone else. Not just anyone else, but someone Athena cared about—her dearest friend, Miss Grace Thomas. This was pure, unrelenting torture. The only good thing was she didn't have to stand next to her friend as she said her vows and married Mason, Earl of Marland."

Miss Evangeline glanced up at him. "Should I read more?"

"This is an odd start to a story. I can see why you said it's about love and loss. The first paragraph says it all." He frowned. "How could she sit through a wedding that devastated her?"

"I'll take that as a yes." She grinned, then started to read again. "Athena had loved Mason since she was but two and ten, when he'd first come to visit her family estate. He was a friend of her brother, Adriel. Her brother had brought his friend home over the holidays. Mason's father had died when he was young, and his mother couldn't be bothered with him. Adriel had felt sorry for his friend, and Athena had fallen in love. He had been a sad boy with dark hair and soft gray eyes. She'd wanted to wrap him up in warmth and bring him as much happiness as possible. In the end, she hadn't been what brought him joy. Grace made him light up. Athena never would, and that hurt more than she ever wanted to admit."

"What is this all about?" a man asked.

Bas had been enthralled listening to Miss Evangeline read. He hadn't heard anyone walk in. He glanced up and met his friend's gaze. "Riverdale," he greeted. "Where's Huntington?"

"Ensuring our trunks are delivered to our chamber." Riverdale gestured toward Miss Evangeline and her book. "Is it story time?"

She closed the book and set it down on a nearby table. "It was," she said. "But it is done for the day." Miss Evangeline smiled at him. "We will pick up where we left off tomorrow. Enjoy your time with your friends." With those words, she left him alone with the duke. Bas cursed under his breath. Their time together had been entirely too short, and damn it, he wanted to know more about this Athena and her lost love. Instead of taking out his mood on his friend, he stood and met Riverdale's gaze. "We have work to do. Let's go find Huntington."

Bas would find Miss Evangeline later. He would

not be able to keep his distance from her, but the mission always came first. He would see it through, and then he'd be free to pursue the only woman he found interesting. Bas couldn't wait to begin that pursuit but for now…he had other priorities. Riverdale followed him out of the library and they went in search of their friend.

HUNTINGTON WAS STROLLING DOWN THE STAIRS when they reached the foyer. He paused at the bottom and glared at two women who were strolling down the hall. Bas should intercede, but he'd learned a long time ago not to get in-between his friends and his cousins. Agatha wasn't his cousin by blood, but they'd all been raised together. Seraphina always came across as abrasive in her dealings with both Riverdale and Huntington, but especially the duke. She could be far kinder to the marquess. He stopped and nodded at them. "Shouldn't you two be socializing with the other ladies?"

Seraphina lifted a brow. "Shouldn't you be somewhere else? Maybe a brothel? The courtesans like you and Riverdale more than we do."

"That's because you don't like anyone,"

Riverdale drawled. "It would mean you have to actually search for a man that is willing to endure your tantrums."

"I do not throw tantrums," Seraphina said defiantly. "You don't like it when a woman has an opinion. You should consider adjusting your standards or you'll never find a willing bride."

"Finding a woman to marry has never been the issue," he said. "It's finding one I want to shackle myself too that is the true dilemma." Riverdale glared at her. "It's lucky I have more of a choice than you do or I'd certainly be as miserable as you are."

"That's enough," Agatha said. "Trading barbs isn't anyone's idea of a fun morning activity."

"That's true enough," Riverdale agreed. "Somerset had a better time than all of us from what I could see."

Bas wanted to strangle the duke. Why did he have to swing the attention back to him? He didn't want any part of this little game of words they were all playing. Agatha had been surprisingly quiet through it all. So had Huntington after the initial volley…was something going on there? No. They had been all avoiding entanglements for far too long for that to have changed now.

"Oh?" Seraphina lifted a brow and then turned toward Bas. "What have you been doing this morning?"

"Nothing important," he replied. His time with Miss Evangeline was his own.

"Don't play the coy young miss," Riverdale teased. "Tell your cousin the truth."

"That is the truth," he said in a tone that suggested he'd murder his friend if he didn't keep his mouth shut. That didn't stop the duke though...

"Perhaps," Riverdale conceded. "But it isn't the entire truth. What are you afraid of?" He tilted his head to the side. "What secrets are you keeping?"

Huntington shook his head and laughed. "More than anyone knows. That's the wrong question to ask."

"The marquess is correct," Agatha said in a soft tone. "Bas is always keeping some sort of secret."

"But this is the only one that involves a woman." Riverdale grinned like the idiot Bas was pretending to be "Tell them about your morning story time."

Bas groaned. "He's making this out to be more than it is."

"Is he?" Seraphina asked. "Were you with Miss Evangeline Payne this morning?" She smiled, and it held a little wickedness. "You don't need to tell us everything. Keep your secrets cousin. I can always uncover them later, and from the little mouse herself."

"Don't pester Miss Evangeline. I told you it wasn't anything important." It had meant everything to him. He turned toward his friends. "However there are things we do need to turn our attention to."

"Run along," Seraphina said. "Agatha and I will seek out your young lady and ensure your intentions are honorable."

Bas held back a groan and chose not to respond. He would have to trust that Miss Evangeline could take care of herself. Agatha and Seraphina were harmless. They would never do anything to intentionally hurt her. The worst that would come of it all would be them discovering the little storybook she had shared with him. There was nothing wrong with that…he hoped.

Six

Eva stared at her teacup and wished she could set it down, then leave the parlor. She had no desire to sit and listen to the chatter of the women that surrounded her. Lady Seraphina Bell and Miss Agatha Cartwright seemed like decent women, but the rest of the guests…well, they had to be the most loathsome individuals she'd ever crossed paths with. Unfortunately for Eva, she had no escape from their vileness. This was her life, and she had to live it. Maybe one day she could do something to change her fate, but for now, she just accepted her lot.

"My maid informed me that the Duke of Riverdale and the Marquess of Huntington arrived earlier today," Lady Dowden said in a shrill tone.

Eva inwardly winced from the sharpness. "I'm certain one of them will find my Jane to their liking."

Eva glanced away from her and rolled her eyes. She hadn't met the Marquess of Huntington, but the Duke of Riverdale hadn't appeared to be a fool, and only one lacking intelligence would willingly tie themselves to a woman like Lady Jane Williams. She doubted the duke was such a man, and the lady would be sorely disappointed.

Lady Seraphina lifted a brow. "That's a presumptuous statement, Lady Dowden." She tilted her head to the side. "Pray tell what is it about your daughter that makes you believe she might snare a duke or a marquess?" She shook her head, then frowned. "Because I must say that I don't see what you do." Eva repressed a smile. Lady Dowden and Lady Jane would not like being so dismissed.

"It must be a mother's pride," Miss Agatha said in an apathetic tone. "I cannot speak from experience, but I've been told that many parents believe their children superior to all others." It was growing increasingly difficult not to smile or laugh at the dressing down Lady Dowden and Lady Jane were receiving.

"You may be right," Lady Seraphina replied to

Miss Agatha. "Is that it, Lady Dowden? Are you feeling an overwhelming sense of pride in your daughter and is that the reason you feel she's superior to all others?"

"You two are the most tiresome women," Lady Dowden replied in a huff. "Did no one teach you two any manners?" There was disgust in her tone as she glared at them.

"I have perfect manners," Lady Seraphina told her in a haughty tone. "Perhaps your own lack of them has made you see something in me that is not there. I can loan you a looking glass if you'd like to actually see what rudeness is."

The more Lady Seraphina and Miss Agatha talked, the more Eva grew to like them. "Would anyone like more tea?" Eva asked. As much as she enjoyed witnessing Lady Dowden being put in her place, Eva didn't wish for her aunt to find a way to blame it on her. Somehow anything that went wrong was Eva's fault. So she had to find a way to diffuse the tension in the room.

"No one wants tea girl," Lady Dowden spat out.

Well, that hadn't gone as planned... "Lady Dowden doesn't wish any tea," Eva said in a neutral tone. "Does anyone else?"

"I would love some," Lady Seraphina said in a pleasant tone. "Thank you, Miss Evangeline."

"Pour me some as well," Miss Agatha replied. "I find I'm positively parched." Her tone dared everyone to suggest she lied.

Eva picked up the teapot and refilled their cups, then sat back down. The two women sipped their tea as Lady Dowden glared at them all. Eva took a small fortifying breath and prayed that a lecture wouldn't be waiting for her later. Lady Dowden might dislike Lady Seraphina, but she wouldn't lay the blame at her feet. As the daughter of a duke she was nearly untouchable. Especially one as affluent as the Duke of Wharton. Sometimes, Eva was jealous of ladies like the duke's daughter. She would have to do something completely scandalous to ruin herself and never be accepted in society. Lady Seraphina had more clout and social standing than Eva ever would have. Other times she was grateful she wasn't scrutinized nearly as much. She had freedom of a different sort. She was a wallflower and mostly unnoticeable. It was both a curse and a blessing.

"Miss Evangeline," Lady Seraphina began. "I heard that you love reading. I was hoping to visit the library. Perhaps you can help me choose a book."

"I would be happy to," she told her. Had her cousin told her about Eva's love of reading? The earl must have… Otherwise how would she have known to ask for her assistance. It made Eva wonder exactly what the earl had said about her. "Do you prefer anything or are you open to suggestions?"

"If I'm being honest I don't like many books. I just like to read before bedtime. It helps me sleep." She flipped her hand nonchalantly. "So anything you recommend will be sufficient. Would you like to walk with me to the library now?"

Eva would like nothing more, but that might not be possible at the moment. She glanced at her aunt for permission. "Go," her aunt said in a dismissive tone. "You're not needed here."

She wasn't going to give her aunt a chance to change her mind. After she went to the library with Lady Seraphina she could hide in her room until dinner. "I would love to walk with you to the library," she said, then stood.

"Lovely," Lady Seraphina replied in a blithe tone. She turned to Miss Agatha. "Will you be joining us?"

"Of course," she answered and lifted her lips into a warm smile. Miss Agatha glanced around the room quickly and then met Lady Seraphina's gaze. "I wouldn't stay here for anything."

The three of them left the parlor and headed toward the library. It wasn't that long ago that Eva had been in there and reading to Lord Somerset. Her time with him had been enjoyable, and she looked forward to the next time she would be able to spend time with him. He wasn't at all unintelligent. Eva liked him more than she had ever liked a gentleman before. She couldn't help wondering why he seemed to pay attention to her. What did he hope to gain?

"Lady Evangeline may I ask you a question," Lady Seraphina said, breaking the silence in their stroll toward the library.

"Of course," Eva answered. She hoped it wouldn't be something she couldn't answer.

"Why do you stay here with them?" She had a perplexed expression on her face. "It's clear you're not of their ilk."

Eva sighed. "My father believes that my aunt can help me find a husband." She didn't add that her father wanted to be rid of her and the sooner the better. Eva was nothing but a burden to her family. She wasn't even sure if her father actually thought Aunt Clara could help her with her marriage dilemma or if he just wanted her gone. As long as he didn't have to see her everyday, he could forget she existed. Eva had no misconceptions about how her father thought about her. She meant nothing. Less than nothing… She doubted he had any real feelings for her at all.

"And the ton believes Somerset an imbecile," Miss Agatha said in a dry tone. "I fear for our world when the likes of Lady Dowden and Lady Andover are at the highest echelons of society."

"Isn't that the truth," Lady Seraphina replied. "It will be up to us to make changes." She turned toward Eva. "I do hope we will be great friends. You seem like a good sort and my cousin likes you. He is the best judge of people and I trust his assessment of you."

"Your cousin?" Eva was confused, then she remembered. She was so overwhelmed she forgot for a brief moment about the earl. How could she have forgotten about him? She had been thinking about him and his relationship to Lady Seraphina a few moments earlier. She was the one being addle brained… "You mean Lord Somerset?"

"Of course," she said in a congenial tone. "I'm

glad you're able to see through this charade he presents to the world. It's good that he has someone like you."

Eva was growing more and more baffled as Lady Seraphina spoke. "I see." But she didn't. What did she hope would happen between Eva and Lord Somerset? What did Lady Seraphina think Eva saw that others didn't?

"I'm glad that you do." She paused at the entrance to the library. "Now show me this book you were reading to him. I must admit when he told me about it I grew quite curious."

They must have a very close relationship for him to have told her about it. "All right," Eva agreed. "But I must insist you return it to me in the morning so I can read to Lord Somerset again." She refused to miss her appointment with him. It was the highlight of her day. Afterward she'd have to succumb to whatever Aunt Clara had planned for her.

She smiled. "I promise it will be here when you're ready. I would hate to disrupt your time together."

Eva shook her head and walked to the shelf an plucked the volume off from where she'd returned it earlier, then gave it to Lady Seraphina. She took the book and sat down on the settee and started to read.

"If you two will excuse me I think I am going to retire to my bedchamber. It's been a taxing afternoon." She had a lot to think about and Eva wanted to do it alone.

"We can take care of ourselves," Miss Agatha replied. "Go and clear your head."

Lady Seraphina was too busy reading to answer. That was fine with Eva because her mind was too muddled for any more polite conversation. Instead she left them alone and went straight to her bedchamber, and blessed silence.

THE EVENING MEAL FELT AS IF IT WERE TAKING AN eternity to finish. All of the guests that Lady Andover invited had finally arrived. Every single one of them were seated at the table. Bas was on Miss Evangeline's right and the Earl of Moray was on her left. The old earl was trying his best to keep her attention solely on him and Miss Evangeline was dodging his attempts better than a gentleman avoiding marriage minded misses.

Bas had to admit he found it all entertaining. He

leaned over slightly and said, "Do you need assistance?"

"With?" she answered in a prim tone.

"Extricating yourself from Moray's attentions of course," he replied drolly.

Her lips twitched but she managed to hold in the giggle that seemed about to burst out of her. "I assure you I am capable of taking care of myself."

"That doesn't mean that you cannot accept the generous help of a gentleman with the best of intentions." His lips tilted upward. Bas really did like her.

She studied him and asked, "Are they?"

"Are they what?" he lifted a brow. Bas was confused. He had been momentarily lost in his own thoughts.

"Are your intentions the best," she said in an earnest tone. "Or are you as bad as others with their lecherous glances and lewd quips."

Bas's mood darkened at her words. "Who is acting that way toward you?" He would have a private word with any gentleman that treated her in such a manner. No, he couldn't do that... It would ruin his carefully crafted cover. He could have Huntington or Riverdale do it for him. After his friends spoke to these dishonorable gentlemen, they wouldn't bother Miss Evangeline Payne ever again. It was the least he could do for her.

She sighed. "You don't need to do that."

"What?" She was making him look like the idiot everyone believed him to be. At this rate she would only add to his reputation. He had to stay focused on their conversation.

"I told you I can take care of myself. You don't need to take care of anyone for me." She pushed the food on her plate around with her fork. He had been watching her all evening and she'd barely touched her food. Instead of asking her again he decided to change the topic of their conversation. He could find out later who was bothering her.

"Do you not like the meal?" he asked. Bas was concerned about her lack of appetite. He hoped that whatever bothered her wasn't something that would continue to weigh on her. If he could help, he would.

She shook her head lightly. "I'm not hungry. The food is all right."

That wasn't much of an answer but what else could he do but accept it. "I personally am not fond of mutton," he explained. "But I was taught to be grateful for any meal at an early age." When his father had been alive, he'd been strict about everything.

"My aunt feels the same. She won't be happy if I don't eat," Miss Evangeline told him. "However, in the same breath she would comment on my lush figure and how I could afford to lose a stone or two."

Bas frowned. "There's nothing wrong with your figure." He liked her lush frame and if he was lucky enough to win her hand in marriage, he would enjoy that delectable body of hers and show her how wonderful it could be between them. "Do not listen to your aunt. She isn't as knowledgeable as she thinks she is." The more he learned about Lady Andover the less he thought of her. She seemed to be a horrid woman, and whenever they spoke she was condescending toward him. Many were, but it always irritated him. They treated him as if he were inferior, despite his title, because they believed him a fool and not worth their consideration. That was why he liked Miss Evangeline. She had always treated him with kindness regardless of what others thought of him.

"I had an interesting conversation with your cousin earlier today," Miss Evangeline said. It was her turn to change their topic of conversation. He smiled but didn't comment on it.

"Did you," he said in a nonchalant tone. "What did you discuss?" The more important question was what scheme did Lady Seraphina concoct?

"She wished to read the book I started earlier today." Miss Evangeline said in a casual tone.

Bas frowned. He shouldn't have let it slip that she had read to him. That had only served to pique Seraphina's curiosity. "Did you tell her about it?"

"I did something better," she replied. "I loaned it to her."

"She's reading it?" He narrowed his gaze. Bas didn't like that at all. "How will you continue to read to me if she has the book?" Seraphina may have ruined his time with Miss Evangeline and Bas didn't like it. He would have words with his cousin.

Her lips quirked upward. Bas liked her smile. "She promised to return it to me in the morning. There's no need to worry, my lord, I will still read to you."

"Good." Because he didn't want to give up any precious time with her. This was as close to courting her that he would get. She was like a rose. Beautiful but with some thorns to protect her. He didn't blame her for putting those sharp edges around herself. With an aunt like Lady Andover she had to do what was necessary. "Then I shall meet you in the library at the same time."

She nodded. "I will be there." There was a promise in her tone that warmed him. She wanted to be with him as much as he wanted to be with her. He would bet everything he owned on that.

He would not miss their scheduled time together. If his meeting later this evening went well with Wharton's contact, he might uncover the smuggling ring and be free of this assignment. Somehow, he doubted that the meeting would be fruitful, or at least make his assignment end sooner anyway. Nothing ever went easy for him, and this task wouldn't be any different.

But one thing would go well—he'd ensure it. Miss Evangeline Payne would read to him, and he would win her. He wanted to be free of Wharton's spying, and she was his key to that. More importantly, she might be the one person he could see as his wife. She was special, and he wouldn't lose his chance with her.

Seven

Bas hated winter. The bitter cold seemed to seep through to his bones and take root. He shivered as a frigid wind rolled around him and enveloped him in an icy gale blanket. Where the hell was Wharton's contact?

He stared out across the cliffs located near Castle Seabury. As cold as it was, he expected there would be frozen waves below, but they rolled to shore as if nothing could stop them from reaching their destination. The distance down to shore was great, and looking downward made Bas's stomach lurch. He wasn't fond of heights and the cliffs was testing his fortitude.

Bas hoped this man showed. Huntington and Riverdale were nearby if he needed them, but he didn't want their assistance unless it was necessary. Bas didn't want to spook Wharton's contact. He needed whatever information the man had, and the sooner the better.

He blew out a frustrated breath. The cold hugged him close and he shivered again. Bas rubbed his hands together to warm them. Why had he forgotten his gloves? Was he losing his ability to think because of one charming female he couldn't stop thinking about? Perhaps. At least she made this trip more enjoyable, and less like the irritating task he'd been given. His uncle would disagree and say his mission held more importance and he should focus on that.

But the more time that passed, the harder that task became. Bas wanted to go back inside. Not just to warm his frozen limbs, but a part of him wished when he did return he'd find her waiting for him. It was a foolish desire and unlikely. The late hour meant she probably had gone to bed hours ago. That was one of the reasons his meeting was taking place in the dead of night. It meant it was less likely he'd cross paths with anyone.

"Lord Somerset," a man said. He had a gruff voice that sounded a little scratchy.

Bas met his gaze. "Who is asking?" He had to

be certain that the man was Wharton's contact. There could be no mistakes. His uncle would be angry if he failed.

The man ran his hand through his dark hair and glanced over the cliffs. That only made Bas more nervous. He turned his attention back to Bas. "Our mutual friend assured me I could trust you. Did he lie?"

"I cannot speak on anyone's behalf. Each person makes their own choices and I cannot control what they may or may not have said." Bas stared at him. "But I know what is expected of me and I always keep my promises."

The man was quiet for several moments. When he spoke again there was resignation in his tone. "I'll have to accept that then." He frowned. "The duke said to tell you everything I've uncovered."

"That is what he told me as well. To expect a report from you." Bas didn't know why the man was stalling but it was starting to irritate him.

"I wish I had more to tell." He started to pace. "I've been working in this cove for a while now. The most I could discover was there was indeed a smuggling ring in this area and it is somehow tied to Castle Seabury."

"But you cannot confirm if the earl is the

leader?" That was not good news. Bas had hoped to have more to work with.

"Correct," the man answered. "Someone in that castle is up to no good. We thought with all the Earl's trips he was the one in charge, but there isn't anything to confirm that."

"Is there any correlation to the smuggling and when he is away?" Bas asked. There had to be something to help him move forward. He hadn't found anything in the earl's study or his chambers. The library was the last place he had to thoroughly search. He'd been interrupted the last time he had tried.

"All I can verify is that when the smugglers are in this area the earl is away. Of course we don't discover that until after the smuggled goods have been dispersed, and then there isn't anything we can do about it."

"If the earl were in charge why would he ensure he was gone when the smugglers were around?" Bas frowned as he considered all of the options. "Wouldn't he want to be here in case of sudden problems? How would he solve those from a distance?"

The man shrugged. "Perhaps he has a second in

command that does that part for him. Most would say he leaves so no one suspects him."

Bas shook his head. "That is always a possibility, but I don't think that is what is happening here."

The person in charge of this smuggling ring was smart and perhaps the reason that they were around when the earl wasn't had more to do with the earl's ability to stop them. Perhaps they were looking at the entire situation all wrong.

"I wish I could have been more help." The man glanced over at the cliffs again. "Is there anything else I can help with?"

He hadn't given Bas much, but he did help him a little. "There's nothing else I need. I'll take it from here." But he had given Bas enough information to make him reconsider how he should proceed with the investigation. He would discuss it with Huntington and Riverdale. They might be able to help him pinpoint what he'd missed.

"Then I'll be off. It's bloody cold out." The man rubbed his hands together, then wandered away from Bas.

After the man was some distance away Huntington and Riverdale joined him. "Do you believe what he told you?" Riverdale asked.

"He has no reason to lie," Bas replied. His uncle seemed to trust him anyway.

"None that you are aware of," Huntington added. "Still… It is interesting that the earl is away when the smugglers are doing business. What do you think it means?"

"That someone close to the earl, one that knows his schedule," Bas began. "Is the real mastermind. I'd say that list is limited." It was the only thing that made any sort of sense. The more he thought about it that possibility seemed the most likely.

"His estate manager, maybe his solicitor," Riverdale added.

"And let's not forget his esteemed wife," Huntington replied. "We should never underestimate the motives of a female. They can be quite cunning at times." The marquess would know that better than anyone. His own experiences with women left him bitter at times.

"Yes…" Bas considered Lady Andover. Could she be this devious? She wasn't a pleasant person, but would she involve herself with smugglers? That seemed something she'd consider beneath her. "We have more investigating to do. Let's head back before our bollocks freeze off."

Huntington and Riverdale laughed but fell into

step beside him. Tomorrow he would have another reading session with Miss Evangeline, but tonight he had more work to do.

EVA COULDN'T SLEEP. SHE COULD NOT GET LORD Somerset off of her mind. When she closed her eyes, he was all that she saw, and when she opened them he still haunted her day dreams. Nothing could erase him from her thoughts and she didn't really want to make them go away. She *liked* him.

Perhaps she should reconsider the rose quartz. He was the first man that she had met that tempted her to use its magic. What if she didn't use it and lost him. Then again, what if she did use it and still lost him… There were so many choices she had to make, and none of them seemed like a good idea.

She rose from her bed and went over to where she had stored the quartz. Eva opened the drawer on her writing desk and pulled it open, then lifted the velvet bag. She pulled the pendant out of the bag and set it in the palm of her hand. It warmed her skin and she was tempted to put it on, to wear it, and let its power aid her in securing her one true love. It had helped two of her cousins in their paths toward true love. According to them she had nothing to worry about. Eva thought they were wrong. Magic, if one believed in it, had a price. That cost was what concerned her.

As much as she wanted to give in and put the necklace on. Eva didn't give in to that urge. Instead she put it back inside the velvet pouch and in the drawer. When the drawer was once again closed a sense of relief poured over her. The rose quartz wasn't for her. The first chance she could she would send it to her cousin—the last of the four of them that wanted a chance to use its magic.

She turned away from her writing desk and then left her room. A book from the library might help her sleep. She didn't bother with a candle to light her way. Seabury was a dark and drafty castle but she'd become accustomed to it in the few weeks she had been residing there. Slowly she made her way down the stairs and to the hall that led to the library. Eva pushed open the door and stepped inside. It was dark, but it didn't take her long to realize she was not alone in the room. Someone taller and much larger than her was there. She took a moment to study the figure. Eva kept her movements light and focused on steadying her breathing. He, and it was most definitely a male, hadn't realized she had entered the room yet. Eva wanted to keep it that way for as long as possible as she discerned what she should do.

The man stopped suddenly and turned. He froze in place, tilting his head as he stared in her direction. Did he see well enough in the dark to realize it was her? She hoped not. Eva resisted the urge to flee. He might chase her and she didn't know what that might result in. "Miss Evangeline?" the man said in a puzzled tone.

"Lord Somerset?" She moved closer relieved it was him and not someone undesirable, like Lord Moray. At least she felt at ease in Lord Somerset's company, and in fact, welcomed the idea of spending time with him. "Why are you in here? Are you looking for another book?" She glanced around. "And why didn't you light a candle?" She hoped he didn't ask her the same question. Eva didn't wish to explain herself.

He looked at the bookshelves and then back at her. "I didn't wish to bother with a candle…too much work. Besides I wasn't certain I actually wanted a book."

"Oh?" She frowned. "Then why come here?" She loved the library and the smell of books, but she didn't think anyone else felt the same way.

Eva moved toward him so she could see his features better. She hadn't come to the library hoping to see him, but now that he was there with her she couldn't help being glad for the coincidence.

He sighed. "I'm having trouble sleeping, and well, you know about my reading difficulties."

She wasn't certain he actually had any difficulties, but she'd continue to play along with him. It might make it easier to discern his motives that way. "I do." Eva frowned. "That doesn't explain why you're here. If reading a book is so tedious why seek out a room filled with them."

"In truth," he began. Lord Somerset fidgeted. It was endearing… "I was reliving our moment earlier in the day. It was nice to envision you there on the settee and your lovely voice as you read from the little red book. It was better than laying in my bed unable to sleep no matter how hard I tried."

Eva could relate to that. Was that the real reason she had sought the library herself. So she could imagine him there with her. If so, wasn't this far better? "I'd read more but your cousin still has the book." And she didn't really wish to light a candle. The darkness had an intimateness that she found exhilarating.

"And she's to return it soon?" His voice was a little husky. He stepped a little closer toward her. Eva's skin heated as he neared.

"Yes," she said in a hushed tone. They were so close now she could almost feel his breath on her skin. "I'll read to you in a few short hours." If she didn't oversleep from her restless night…

"I cannot wait," he said. His mouth was so close to her ear that she could feel the words as he spoke them. They vibrated through her. "I find even the smallest amount of time with you is both enjoyable and frustrating. When you leave I want to seek you and when you're here I fear you'll have to leave. It's a conundrum I cannot escape."

"I enjoy our time together too," she admitted. Eva lifted her head and turned it to meet his gaze. "What is happening here?" Her voice was hoarse with emotion.

He placed his hands on her cheeks and stared into her eyes. "I don't know," he began. "But I know one thing. I cannot allow this to end. You, Miss Evangeline, have woven a spell around me and even if it could be broken I'd never wish it so."

She swallowed hard. "I'm no witch."

He smiled. "No," he agreed. "You're much more vibrant that that. You my dear, are a siren, and your very presence makes me sing with joy." Lord Somerset lowered his head until his lips touched hers. The kiss was tentative at first, but then passion overtook him. He deepened the kiss and then wrapped his arms around her, crushing her against him.

It was devastating. It was everything. Eva couldn't get enough, and she lost all ability to reason, and let herself fall. She had once had some mead. It hadn't tasted dangerous when she drank it, but after drinking half her glass she reached for it and missed. The effects had sneaked up on her and overtaken her senses. This kiss was like that. At first it had seemed light and quickly turned her upside down. She no longer controlled herself, her innate nature had taken over, and that part of her wanted everything Lord Somerset had to offer her. Eva's fate was in his hands now, and she prayed she wouldn't live to regret it.

Breaking that kiss had felt as if something integral had been ripped away from her, but it had to be done. Lord Somerset had been the one to do it. Eva didn't have the strength to sever their tie. His breathing was heavy, and so was hers.

"We should stop…" He brushed his hand over her hair. Her skin was on fire and craved his touch.

"I want you so damn much…but this isn't the time or the place."

She nodded unable to speak. What was he doing to her?

"Go," he said. His voice was hoarse as he spoke. "Before I do something unwise." He kissed her cheek. "I'll see you in the morning."

Eva didn't want to leave him but understood why he wanted her to. Her reputation and his would suffer if anyone found them in an intimate embrace. The very fact they were alone, and she only wore her nightdress and wrapping gown would be enough to ruin her. She reluctantly turned away from him and left the library. It was the most difficult thing she'd ever done, but somehow she managed to walk back to her bedchamber and crawl back into her bed.

Eight

Eva woke with a start. Her heart raced inside of her chest and it felt as if she had been running. She scanned her bedchamber to see what had made her wake, but there was nothing there. It was well past dawn and sun had started to stream in through the window. She rarely slept so late.

Last night… Images of the kiss she had shared with Lord Somerset came flooding through her mind in vivid detail. She touched her lips tentatively. That had really happened, and she wanted to find a way to entice the earl to kiss her again. It had been the single most thrilling moment in her entire life.

She swung her legs over the side of her bed. The faster she dressed the quicker she could meet with him in the library. She paused momentarily… Seraphina still had the book. Eva would have to retrieve the volume from her first. Hopefully she wouldn't be difficult to locate.

Eva dressed in a simple blue muslin gown, then slid her arms into a spencer for some added extra warmth. It was a dark blue wool that emphasized the light blue gown. After she dressed, she paused a moment and glanced back at her writing desk. She couldn't explain why, but she had to open the drawer and check on the rose quartz. Eva still hadn't written to her cousin so she could send the rose quartz to her. She should do that as soon as possible. Once the rose quartz was no longer in her possession, she'd feel much better.

She opened the drawer and reached inside, but nothing was there. Eva stared at the empty drawer. Where was it? Panic started to fill her and her heart began to race again. Was this what had awakened her? Had she sensed someone in the room? She had to find the rose quartz. If she didn't send it to her cousin… She swallowed hard. How could she possibly explain to her that she'd lost the rose quartz? Of the four of them, everyone would have had a chance with it except the final cousin. It wasn't fair, but if Eva didn't locate that pendant that would be the reality. Somehow she had to find it…Eva couldn't disappoint her cousin.

A knock echoed through her bedchamber. She took a deep breath and then hollered, "Come in." She didn't care who was on the other side of the door. Eva had more important things on her mind. Perhaps she hadn't put it in the drawer. What if she dropped it? She fell to her knees and started to look under the desk. She ran her fingers over the carpet, but there was no blue velvet pouch, and there was definitely no rose quartz pendant.

"Miss Evangeline," a woman said from behind her.

Eva sat up and glanced over her shoulder. "Lady Seraphina," said a little breathlessly. "Miss Agatha. What can I help you with?" Both ladies were staring down at her.

"Seems as if that is something we should be asking you," Miss Agatha replied. "Did you misplace something?"

"I'm not certain…" Eva frowned. She didn't want to tell them about the rose quartz. Explaining a magic pendant did not seem like a prudent idea. "That is I thought I placed it in this drawer, but it isn't there."

"So you thought perhaps it fell on the floor," Lady Seraphina added.

Eva nodded. "Yes," she told her. "But I'm afraid it isn't there either." Disappointment flooded her. *Drat.* Where could it be?

That stupid rose quartz. She should have passed it on to her cousin immediately. Eva had known she didn't want anything to do with that bloody pendant. Now it was missing, and she would have to explain how she'd lost it. She was so mad at herself for being so unresolved what to do with it. If she had followed her instincts she wouldn't be desperately searching for it now.

"What exactly did you misplace?" Miss Agatha asked. "If we are to assist you we need to know what to look for."

Eva sighed. She didn't want to explain the rose quartz. They might think her a little mad to believe in such things as magic. Even one that aided you while it cursed you… "I have a pendant in a blue velvet pouch. It's a family heirloom…it belonged to my grandmother." There. That should be a sufficient explanation.

"What does the pendant look like?" Lady Seraphina asked. "If it was stolen the thief may attempt to wear it."

She gasped. "Do you actually believe they would dare such a thing?" They might regret wearing it too. She didn't think anyone knew about the rose quartz or the story behind it—that was a family secret. Who would want to steal it?

Miss Agatha shrugged. "Some people can be quite brazen." She turned toward Miss Seraphina. "We should ask the shrewd three for assistance."

"The shrewd three?" Eva lifted a brow.

"Somerset, Huntington, and Riverdale," Lady Seraphina said nonchalantly. "Come with us. I know where to find them. You can describe the pendant to them. They're more likely to know how to locate it than us. It's what they do."

Eva didn't know how she felt about this development. What exactly did the three gentlemen do to be deemed the shrewd three? She would have to ask Lord Somerset about that. She suddenly felt as if she didn't know him that well at all. There was still very much she needed to learn about him.

"You truly think that is the best solution?" she asked the two of them.

"It is," Lady Seraphina said in a firm tone.

"Here." She handed the red book to her. "This is why we came to your bedchamber. It was a delightful read. I can see why Somerset was pleased with it."

In all the chaos Eva had forgotten about the book and reading to Lord Somerset. She wasn't certain she would be able to read to him. Not if she wanted time to search for her lost pendant. She hoped he would understand why she might have to postpone their reading time. "Thank you," she said to Lady Seraphina. "I wouldn't want to misplace this too." She should keep it with her in case the thief thought to steal it as well.

Lady Seraphina smiled. "Don't worry. Your pendant will be found. If I know Somerset he won't give up until it is with you again." She nodded at Miss Agatha. "Follow me. We have work to do."

With that the three of them left the bedchamber to go in search of the shrewd three. That still felt odd to even think about…

Bas wanted to kiss Miss Evangeline again. He didn't know when he would get the chance, but he wouldn't let it slip away once he had it. She was supposed to read more to him. He was in the library but she had yet to show. Huntington and Riverdale were still there with him. They would make themselves scarce once she arrived though.

"What are you thinking about?" Riverdale asked him.

"Nothing," he said absentmindedly. He stared out the window and watched snow fall to the ground. It was a good thing none of them had plans to travel. It appeared as if they were going to get quite a bit of the white substance.

"Why don't I believe you," Riverdale said. His tone held a hint of humor in it. "You're thinking about her aren't you?"

Bas was but he wouldn't admit that to Riverdale. His friend would take that fact and use it against him. Not in a bad way, but in a mocking one. He didn't want to listen to his friend poke fun at him. "Not at all," he replied in a smooth tone. "Do you think we will get a lot of snow?" He supposed it would be nice to have it covering the ground for Christmas…not that he wanted to spend the season at this particular castle.

"Changing the topic of conversation is a sure sign you were thinking about a certain lady," Huntington drawled. "You forget we know you."

Bas closed his eyes and blew out a breath. "Then you also know that I have no desire to discuss it."

"She means that much to you?" Riverdale lifted a brow. "All right. We will let it be. For now."

A reprieve was better than nothing. Bas would accept that concession and hope it lasted long enough for him to finish this last task for his uncle. "Did you two discover anything useful after our meeting last night?"

"No," Huntington replied. "I was going to travel to the nearby town but this weather is going to prevent that. It will have to wait a couple of days."

Bas cursed under his breath. He had just been thinking it was a good thing they didn't need to go anywhere in the current weather conditions. He hadn't considered the case when he had that thought. This was not good. "Well, there's no helping that I suppose. We will just have to continue to investigate what we can here and hope something turns up."

"I don't know how much more we will find here," Riverdale said. "And the company has been…"

"A bit much," Huntington supplied. He sighed

and then frowned. "That Lady Jane is quite brazen. She won't stop touching me." He shuddered. "I cannot wait to depart this drafty old castle."

Bas laughed. "I thought you liked attention from ladies."

"Not ones like that," Riverdale said and glared at him. "She actually let her hand slip so it grazed my arse. She is acting like a courtesan in training. I'm with Huntington…the sooner I can leave the better." Bas didn't think brazen was the right word for that sort of action…she sounded more desperate than anything. Why?

"You might not like pretending to be stupid," Huntington began. Irritation was laced through his words as he spoke. "But at least the marriage minded ladies leave you be. That my friend is a blessing."

Until the time came for him to find a wife… Miss Evangeline Payne was special, and he hoped to court her more, then convince her to marry him. It will take a lot for many members of society to accept he wasn't addle-brained, and some might never see him as intelligent. None of that mattered as long as he had a wife as wonderful at Miss Evangeline Payne.

He didn't get a chance to reply thankfully. As

soon as he opened his mouth to speak his cousin, Lady Seraphina waltzed into the library. Miss Agatha and Miss Evangeline followed behind her.

"I'm glad you're all still here." His cousin headed over to his side. "We need your help."

"How novel of you," Riverdale drawled. "I thought you didn't need anyone's assistance."

She turned toward the duke and glared at him. "I don't." The animosity between Seraphina and Riverdale was so thick it made the room suffocating. Bas really wished his friend and his cousin could learn to be more civil with each other.

"But you just said…" Riverdale began to say.

Lady Seraphina didn't give him a chance to reply. "The help isn't for me. Let me clarify." She turned her attention back to Bas—blatantly ignoring the duke. "Miss Evangeline needs you."

Bas's heart skipped a beat at her words. He would do anything for Miss Evangeline. He focused his attention on her. She was dressed in all blue and she looked so pretty it almost hurt to look at her. The little red book was in her hands. She hadn't forgotten her promise to read more to him. "What is wrong?" he asked in a gentle tone.

She opened her mouth to speak but Seraphina

spoke first. "Someone stole her grandmother's necklace from her. You must help her find it."

"Why do you think I can locate it?" They had told Seraphina several times not to let anyone know what he did. Now she was claiming he could help Miss Evangeline uncover a thief. He would have to speak to her again in private.

"I'm sure your two friends can add some valuable assistance." She didn't once glance at Riverdale. The two of them fought more often than not. It made Bas think there was something more going on between them, but he didn't ask. Agatha had not said a word since she entered, but it was not lost on him how she sneaked glances of Huntington. Were his two friends oblivious or were they keeping the two ladies at a distance for a reason?

"I'm certain they can help." He glanced at Miss Evangeline. "I assume this pendant is important to you?"

She met his gaze. There was wariness in her eyes that unsettled him. "It is. I was going to send it to my cousin...we...we..." She stopped a minute and took a deep breath. "We share it and its her turn to have it. I must find it."

"Then we shall," he said. Bas stepped forward and placed her hands in his. "You have my word that it will be returned. No one should have taken it from you." A family heirloom that was shared around seemed important…they all must have wanted it and this was their solution. He could ask her for more details later in that regard.

He would need more information about the heirloom. Such as where she'd kept it and how valuable it was, but for now he wanted to comfort her. She appeared so distraught. "Tell me everything," he said and led her to the settee. Once she was settled he sat beside her and waited for her to speak. He took in every detail and after she was finished he smiled. "If you think of anything else let me know immediately. I don't want you to worry."

"Because this is what you do?" she asked, then glanced at Huntington and Riverdale. "The shrewd three?"

He cursed under his breath. Bas was definitely going to have to talk with Seraphina and Agatha. One of them must have let that tidbit slip. "Something like that," he said. "Now I assume we are going to postpone our reading time."

"If..if.." She glanced away as if embarrassed, then took a deep breath. "If you don't mind."

"Of course I don't." He wanted to pull her into his arms and ease her worries. "I'll find you later."

Bas stood and nodded at Huntington and Riverdale. They rose and followed him out of the library. They solved mysteries and were master spies. They would uncover that bloody smuggling ring, and he would find Miss Evangeline's pendant. No one *hurt* her and got away with it.

Nine

Tomorrow was Christmas day, but later that night was the ball Eva's aunt had planned. The house party would end soon and they still had not found the rose quartz. She didn't know what she would do if she didn't locate it soon or at all... It had to still be in the castle. No one had left and that implied the thief was still there. At least in theory... What did Eva know about thievery or people that felt the need to steal. Nothing. Absolutely nothing.

She sighed. It was time to return to her chamber to prepare for the ball. Her gown had been delivered the day before and she had to admit her aunt had commissioned her a lovely dress. It was a rich vermilion velvet trimmed with a silver lace around the bodice and a matching spencer. She couldn't have picked out a more perfect gown if she'd tried.

Eva sighed and stood. She had hoped that Lord Somerset would come to the library and she could speak with him before she had to go upstairs. It was time to give up on that notion. She headed toward the door and stopped when she heard voices. Two women were speaking in the hallway. Their voices were slightly raised.

"Don't argue with me girl," Lady Dowden said in a harsh tone. "You forget your place."

"Mother," Lady Jane said in a dismissive tone.

"And don't roll your eyes at me." Lady Dowden sounded quite irritated with her daughter…

Why were they arguing? What had Lady Jane done that made her mother so annoyed at her? Eva didn't want them to realize she was there. They were unpleasant on a good day, and if they knew she'd unintentionally eavesdropped they would certainly be unkind. She nearly snorted. Unkind indeed. They'd be horrifyingly terrible toward her.

"We're only here for a few more days. Are you any closer to securing a match with Huntington or Riverdale?" Lady Dowden asked.

"They're slipperier than a fish out of water," Lady Jane said.

"And what would you know about fish and water," Lady Dowden scoffed. "Quit giving me excuses. I expect one of them to propose to you tonight. I want to announce your betrothal at the Christmas Ball."

"I can't make them marry me," Lady Jane whined. Her tone pierced Eva's poor suffering ears… "They don't even seem to like me."

Eva didn't think anyone liked Lady Jane or her mother. She should warn Huntington and Riverdale about this scheme, but she doubted they hadn't discerned the truth already. Still…she'd make a point to speak to at least one of them later.

"They don't have to like you." Lady Dowden told her daughter. "They just have to be willing to make you their wife. We are broke and the smuggling has only touched the surface of our debt. If you don't marry one of them we will be destitute before the season begins."

Smuggling? What were they doing? They didn't act like two people on the brink of ruin, and yet… they were. Eva was starting to realize just how entertaining eavesdropping could be. She couldn't wait to share this information with Lady Seraphina and Miss Agatha. They would probably find it as interesting as she did.

"I did manage to pilfer a few trinkets from the guests," Lady Jane said. "I can sell them when we go to town."

"They won't garner much, but it will help." Lady Dowden sighed. "Trap one of those gentlemen. I would even accept a proposal from that imbecile Lord Somerset. Just find a husband and do it tonight. All of them are rich enough to save us from ruin—any of them will do."

"Yes, Mother," Lady Jane said in a sullen tone. "I'll seduce them if necessary."

"There's my good girl." Lady Dowden's voice was practically beaming with pride. "Now let's go prepare for the evening. You must look your best."

Eva waited several minutes to make sure that they were gone before leaving the library. She had a decision to make. Should she dress before seeking Lord Somerset or find him now and tell him what she'd learned? After a moment of thought she decided to dress first. The countess and her daughter were not going anywhere. They were dressing for the ball first too. It wouldn't take Eva long to prepare, and she would have more time to converse with Lord Somerset if she waited.

With that decision made she went up to her bedchamber. Once there she washed and then set to styling her hair. She didn't have a maid to help her do most things. Her aunt hadn't deemed it a necessity. That had been fine with Eva, but at the moment she wished she could have had one. The sooner she was dressed the quicker she could seek out Lord Somerset.

It would be all right. She had to believe that. At least she now knew who had stolen her pendant. Once she was certain Lady Jane was in the ballroom she could search her bedchamber.

Eva finished her hair and dressed in her ballgown, then went downstairs. She prayed that Lord Somerset was already there and she wouldn't have to search for him.

BAS SAT IN THE CARD ROOM LISTENING TO SOME OF the guests droll on. The ball had begun an hour ago, and a lot of the gentlemen had immediately retreated to the card room. There were some ladies there, but the large part were men. So that is where

Bas had headed. He believed the answers he sought would be found there. At least he hoped so. The house party ended in two days and still he hadn't uncovered the head of the smuggling ring.

"Somerset," a man called. "Come join the game. I could use someone willing to lose a few pounds to me."

"I don't know," Bas said in a tone that made him appear as unintelligent as the man presumed him to be. He bumbled around a bit. "I lose count easily and usually squander too much when I play."

"I know," the man said and laughed. "That's why we want you to join us."

Bas would give anything to punch that smirk off of the man's face. It was Viscount Redding. He was an arrogant arse and believed he was better than almost anyone. "Maybe Huntington will play." He gestured toward the marquess. "I heard he was looking for a good game."

Redding scowled. Huntington was known to win more often than losing. He wouldn't willingly invite the marquess to play. "If he wants to join he can," Redding said a little belligerently.

Huntington made his way over to him. "Gentlemen," he greeted them all. Then leaned a little closer to Bas and said, "Your lady is looking for you."

"Is she?" He lifted a brow. Bas wanted to see her too, but he still had a mission to complete. "Did she tell you that?"

"Not at all," Huntington drawled. "But she is definitely looking for something and it isn't difficult to discern what that something is."

He cursed under his breath. Bas had to go see her. Maybe then he could concentrate on his task. "Can you handle this." He gestured toward the card game.

"I *love* cards," Huntington said then grinned. He turned toward Redding. "Deal me in."

Redding groaned but did as Huntington asked. Bas took that as his cue to leave. If there was anything to learn, Huntington would uncover it. He slid out of the card room and then walked toward the ball. The musicians were playing a quartet and dancers were twirling around the floor.

Bas walked around the room looking for Miss Evangeline. When he finally found her he had to stop to catch his breath. She looked like an angel wrapped in crimson velvet. The dress hugged her bosom in a way that made him itch to touch her. He squeezed his hands into fist to hold the urge back. He walked toward her and she turned as he approached. Bas bowed. "May I have the next dance."

"Dance?" She smiled. "I'd love to."

He held out his hand to her and led her to the floor. The quartet had ended and the musicians were starting the first notes of a waltz. Bas was one lucky man. He placed his hand on her waist and held her other hand in the proper position. When she settled her hand on his shoulder he began the steps. They glided across the floor with ease. Almost as if they'd been dance partners their entire life...a matched pair.

"Lord Somerset," she began—her tone a bit breathless.

He interrupted her, "Bas. Please call me Bas. I think we're beyond formality now."

"Are we?" She lifted a brow but smiled none-theless. "I suppose that is true. Then you must call me Eva."

He smiled. "Eva." He let her name slide off his tongue and liked it. "I never expected to find a woman like you here."

"What did you expect then?" Her gaze never left his as he led them through the steps of the waltz. He saw nothing but her, and it appeared the same was true of her.

He would have shrugged if they hadn't been dancing. "I had no expectations. It was nice to be pleasantly surprised."

Bas wanted her to be his wife. He had never been more certain of something. If only he didn't have this mission hanging over his head…then he could court her properly and ask for her hand.

"You surprised me too." She glanced over to the right of the ballroom, then frowned. "But there's something I need to tell you."

"What is it?" Concern filled him at her words.

"I overheard something earlier," she began. "I know who took my pendant."

He wished he had been able to find that for her. Bas hated that he had failed her. Perhaps he could rectify that now. "Who?" He would handle retrieving her necklace for her. A thief could be violent if cornered, and he didn't want her to be hurt.

"It's about more than the pendant," Eva said. She bit down on her bottom lip and he almost groaned at the sight. "They're scheming and I'm afraid they might succeed if they're not stopped."

"I think you're going to have to tell me everything." The notes of the waltz were starting to die down. "Meet me in the library in a quarter hour. If you see Riverdale tell him to join us."

She nodded her head. "All right."

He led her away from the floor and then went to the library. Bas would wait for her there. Once she told him everything perhaps he could finish this mission. He wasn't certain what she had to tell him, but he had a feeling she had all the answers he'd been seeking. Bas couldn't explain it… Sometimes his intuition told him something and it had never failed him before. He had learned to trust his instincts, and didn't see any reason not to now.

Once he was in the library he made sure a fire was lit in the hearth, then settled onto the settee to wait for her, and hopefully Riverdale too.

"You're not the one I was hoping to find here," a woman said. "But as my mother said, even *you'll* do."

He glanced toward the door and frowned. Lady Jane Williams was walking inside. What the bloody hell was this harpy up to. "Pardon?" He lifted a brow. She had to leave, and fast.

"Don't worry," she said in a sultry tone. "It'll be good I promise."

She sat down beside him on the settee and ran

her hand across his leg. The hussy was intent on seducing him. She was in for a rude awakening, because there wasn't a chance in hell of him succumbing to her wiles. So much for his supposed stupidity keeping her from seeking him out. Bas groaned, and not in pleasure. His friend had cursed him…

Ten

Eva went in search of Riverdale. When she found him she approached him as nonchalantly as she could. "Your Grace," she greeted him. "May I have a word with you?"

He smiled then held out his arm to her. "Perhaps a stroll?"

The Duke of Riverdale was one of the most sought-after guests at the house party. There were several young ladies that glared at her when the duke gave her his attention. None of them realized that the duke had no real interest in her, and she had none in him. Her heart belonged to Bas, and if he asked her to, she'd marry him in a heartbeat.

"Am I correct in assuming you have some information to share with me of the upmost importance?" the duke drawled. His eyes nearly twinkled in delight. Did the possibility of danger excite him?

Eva nodded gravely. "Bas…Lord Somerset that is, asked me to find you."

He lifted a brow. "Did he? That's interesting." The duke led her away from the ballroom. They slipped out and into a hallway. "Where is he?"

"The library," she said. Then frowned when it occurred to her what the shrewd three might be colluding about. "Are you here to find smugglers?"

He laughed so suddenly it startled her. "You're a bright one aren't you? I can see why he likes you." The duke started walking down the hall, then stopped to glance at her. "Are you coming with me?"

It hadn't gone beyond her notice that he hadn't actually answered her. The duke was sly and sneaky. "I'm sure you're aware that Lady Jane is hoping to trap you into marriage."

"Only me?" His tone was filled with disgust. "I think that one will take any willing rich gentleman. She seems quite desperate." The duke glanced at her. "Don't tell me you're worried about me? You needn't be. I've been dodging scheming females for a while now. Huntington and I are quite good at it."

They reached the library and Riverdale pushed

open the door. When they walked in Bas was walking backwards as Lady Jane pursued him.

"Lady Jane," he said in a wary tone. "You need to stop right now. I don't like this. You're not the woman I want."

"I can be," she said in a wantonly. "If you allow it."

"Aww," Riverdale said. "You have a paramour Somerset. I never thought I'd see the day."

Bas glared at him as he dodged Lady Jane. "A little help please," he demanded.

Eva tugged Riverdale's jacket. "She's working with her mother. They're stealing from guests and are part of a smuggling ring." She wanted to wait to tell both of them at the same time, but she didn't like how Lady Jane was eying Bas.

"Is that so?" Riverdale grinned. "You're a font of information." He sighed. "I suppose I will have to assist him then."

"Please do," she said in a stern tone.

Riverdale went over to Lady Jane and lifted her up, then carried her over to a chair by the desk in the room. He sat her down in it. "Stay," he ordered as if she were a dog he demanded to heel.

"You can't do this to me," she said in a shrill tone. "I'm the daughter of an earl."

Somerset came to stand beside Riverdale. "Was that necessary? She's a little slip of a girl."

"Ask her about the smuggling," Riverdale said in response. "and the stealing."

Lady Jane's face went white at Riverdale's words. "I don't know anything."

Eva joined them. "I want my pendant back."

"I don't have it. I swear." She went to stand up and Riverdale pushed her back into the chair. "I don't," she insisted. "At least not anymore. I gave it to my mother."

"I'll handle it." Riverdale turned toward Bas.

"Huntington is in the card room," Bas told him. With that bit of information Riverdale exited the library. Presumably in search of Huntington and the countess.

Bas nodded and then turned his attention back to Lady Jane. Eva was fascinated with this turn of events. It was like seeing a different side of him. She had so many questions, but she knew it wasn't the time to ask.

Bas's features hardened as he faced Lady Jane. "I need you to tell me everything."

She stared at him as if seeing him for the first time. "You're not stupid are you?" Bas was a skilled actor... Eva had known something was off, but now she saw him clearly. His intelligence was there if one thought to look for it, but he kept a part of himself held back no matter what. As if he feared rejection.

He grinned and it was menacing in its intensity. "What do you think?"

"You're not," she said, but not to him to herself. "How could I have not seen it before?"

Eva wondered how anyone could have believed Bas was unintelligent. She had noticed his astuteness the moment she first spoke with him. Why did he act as if he didn't understand anything? What was the purpose of it all?

"Tell me about the smugglers," Bas demanded.

"I don't know much," Lady Jane began. "That's my mother's doing. I..I..." She swallowed hard. "I did steal from the guests. It's not fun being poor. I can't live that way."

"You expect me to feel sorry for you?" Bas scoffed. "I see how you treat people. How you treated Eva." He gestured toward her. "Then you felt it was all right to steal a family heirloom from her?" He shook his head the disgust evident in his features. "No. I don't feel sorry for you. A woman like you doesn't even deserve pity."

"What is going to happen to me?"

"That's not up to me to decide." Bas stepped away and rubbed his hand over his face. He turned to Eva. "I have to take her and her mother to London. My uncle is going to want to talk to them."

"Your uncle?" She lifted a brow. "The Duke of Wharton?"

"Yes," he said. "But this…" He gestured between them. "Is real. I want more with you. I'd like to court you proper."

Her heart filled with joy, but then it sank just as fast. "I don't know if I have time for that. My aunt is arranging a betrothal between me and the Earl of Moray."

"That old man." He glowered. "I'll be back as soon as I can. Try to stop that." He picked her hand up in his. "Please."

Eva nodded. "I'll do my best. I cannot make any promises. You've met my aunt."

He nodded. "I have, and I know what I'm asking of you. Please do your best." He cupped her cheek in his hand briefly. "I'll see your pendant is returned to you after we retrieve it from Lady Dowden."

"Thank you," she said a little overwhelmed. "I'm going to let you finish this."

Eva smiled at him and then turned to leave the

library. She hoped he returned in time, but she had a feeling he wouldn't. Her aunt was determined that she marry Moray. She wouldn't believe that the Earl of Somerset wanted to court her, and even if she did she wouldn't care. Her aunt wanted results, and without Bas around to back her up, that meant it wasn't real. Besides she thought Bas was an imbecile. Why would she approve the match?

BAS HAD DELIVERED LADY DOWDEN AND HER daughter to his uncle. Lady Dowden had been corresponding with Lady Andover regularly to ensure she was aware of the Earl of Andover's comings and goings from Castle Seabury. It was the perfect alibi for her. No one would have suspected her and if she hadn't slipped up, they would still be scrambling to uncover who led the ring.

The smuggling ring had all been arrested. All the stolen jewelry and trinkets returned to their owners, and Lady Dowden and her daughter were probably going to be sent to Australia. Bas honestly didn't care what happened to them. He only had one concern. Eva.

He was riding at a breakneck speed to return to

her. There was only so much distance he could take before he had to switch horses or rest his. As a result it had taken him almost a fortnight to return to Castle Seabury. When he walked into the parlor he found Lady Andover, Eva, and Lord Moray there.

"Ladies," he greeted them. "Lord Moray."

"What brings you back to Castle Seabury, Lord Somerset?" Lady Andover asked.

"I came for Eva," he said in a firm tone.

"Eva?" Lady Andover glanced toward her. "I didn't realize you were so familiar with my niece. What are your intentions?" Lady Andover stared at him in expectation.

"Only the most honorable." He met Eva's gaze. Bas prayed he wasn't too late. "If she'll have me that is."

"You're not the only one vying for her hand." Lady Andover gestured toward the Earl of Moray. "Why should she have you instead?"

Bas clenched his hands at his side. Punching Moray would not aid his cause. Eva was a desirable woman. He didn't blame Moray for wanting to marry her. "Because I love her."

"Love is for fools," Lady Andover said, then waved her hand dismissing him. "It doesn't surprise me that you would believe in such a thing. You're not known for your intelligence." He hated so many thought less of him.

"Don't talk to him that way," Eva told her aunt. There was anger in her eyes as she glanced toward the older woman. "He's not stupid. If anyone is, it's you for not seeing him for who he is."

"Do not address me in that tone." Lady Andover glared at her niece. Then she turned to him. "Give me a better reason than love or I'm giving her to Moray."

Bas clenched his hands tightly at his side. He knew this would not be easy, but he hadn't thought she'd be so blatantly against him either.

"Do that and I'll just kidnap her and take her to Scotland. I'm not letting you give her to a man that will not appreciate her and treat her like the wonderful, brave, loving woman she is." Bas would not lose her.

Lady Andover grinned. "I think I like you." She stood. "I will give you a few moments alone. If my niece agrees to marry you when I return, I will write her father and let him know of her betrothal. Use your time wisely. She still does have options and doesn't need to choose you if she doesn't wish to. I may seem harsh, but I do only have her best interests at heart." She turned toward Moray and ordered, "Walk with me."

He didn't need to convince Eva. At least he didn't think he did… Still he was grateful for the time alone with her. Once Lady Andover and Lord Moray were out of the room Bas dropped to his knees before her. "Eva," he began. "I'm a better man when I'm with you. The second I see you I lose all ability to think or to speak, and I am constantly in awe of you." He placed his hands on hers. "The moment I first met you, and when you offered to read to me, I knew you were the only woman for me. I love you more than I can ever say. Please be my wife."

"I thought you wanted to court me." Her voice held no emotion as she spoke, and it worried him. Did she not want to be with him?

"I do," he said. "I would if there was time. But your aunt…" He glanced toward the door. "She's not going to allow us that luxury." Eva herself had said as much before he left. Why was she being difficult now?

"Did I ever tell you the significance of the rose quartz?" She still seemed a bit off. What was he missing?

"Your pendant?" He was confused. "No, you

didn't. You did say it belonged to your grandmother but didn't elaborate." He had wanted to ask her more about it but so much had happened afterwards…

She nodded. "It led her to her true love. It's said that if you have it you will find your true love. It has a cost and I was afraid to use it. That's why I kept it in the drawer and refused to wear it." Eva glanced away from him. "I think it still led me to you though."

"Do you still have it?" he asked.

Eva shook her head. "No. I sent it to my cousin. It's her turn."

"Are you afraid of what might happen?" He didn't like to see her filled with so much anxiety.

She shook her head. "No. Not anymore. I've been fighting myself for so long." Eva's lips wobbled. "I have let fear control me. I was the one standing in my way. It's time I stopped doing that and accept that something good can happen."

"You'll marry me?"

A tear slipped down her cheek. "There's not enough hours in the day for me to have with you, let alone a lifetime of them. When I close my eyes your all I dream of. You're everything I wanted but never dared wish for. I'll spend the rest of my life learning all I need to about you, and even then I don't know if that will be enough. We don't need to court. We're going to have many years for that."

"I promise you won't regret marrying me."

"I intend to ensure you keep that promise." Eva told him, then grinned. "I love you."

He let out a breath he hadn't realized he'd been holding. "You're right. We might not ever learn everything about each other, but I'm going to try. I'm going to love you every moment of it too."

Bas sat down on the settee with her and pulled her into his arms. Then he pressed his lips to hers. The kiss was sweet and tender, but then quickly turned to something hotter and more passionate. He could finally be the man he was always meant to be, and he had a woman he was proud to have by his side. There was nothing else he could possibly ask for, except perhaps some children so they could have a family to share their love with. He was blessed.

Epilogue

Christmas, the following year…

Eva had a present, the best of presents, for her husband. She couldn't wait to give him his gift. Their one year anniversary was coming soon too. They hadn't wanted to wait long to start their lives together, and her father hadn't argued against a fast wedding. As far as he was concerned she could have moved to Somerset Abby without the benefit of marriage—if that wouldn't have stained his own reputation in the process.

Her issues with her father were best left in the past though. She didn't interact with him at all, and she didn't miss him either. Eva had accepted it wasn't a relationship she could repair. They didn't have a relationship to mend. Her father had never loved her.

She had a new family. One that accepted her and loved her as she'd always dreamed of. Bas was the most important person in that new family. His uncle and cousins had accepted her completely. All of them had agreed to come to Somerset Abby for Christmastide. It was her first one that was filled with happiness. She had decorated the abbey with all the frippery that went with the season— including mistletoe and boughs of holly.

Their guests were all close friends and family. They didn't want to celebrate with anyone that didn't accept them. Bas didn't need to pretend to be less than intelligent anymore, but there were still some in the ton that didn't want to believe he wasn't stupid, and Eva didn't want to subject him to their ridicule. Even if he could dress them down with expert precision.

"Bas," she called out. "Are you in here?"

She strolled into the library and found him flipping through that red book she'd read to him a year ago. He glanced up and held it out to her. "I thought we could read this again."

Eva grinned and walked over to him. She settled on the settee next to him and placed her head on his shoulder. He wrapped his arm around her waist and kissed her temple. "How about you read it this time," she said. "It's your turn to tell me a story."

He still had some difficulty reading. But this story was one he knew well enough to read without it hampering him. They didn't know why he mixed the words up, but that didn't prevent him from trying to enjoy books. He had decided that it was time to stop allowing his fears to dictate his decisions anymore. Over time he was getting better at overcoming his trouble with the words. "But you tell it so well," he said in a seductive tone.

"Your using that voice again," she said. "It doesn't work on me anymore." It still did… "I've adapted to it's potency."

"Then I have to try harder don't I." He leaned down and said huskily into her ear. "Please read to me."

She sighed. "I have a better idea." Eva slid into his lap and wrapped her arms around his neck. "Why don't you join me upstairs." She leaned down. "And we can spend the afternoon alone. No one to interrupt us, and after, if you've earned it… I'll let you have your gift early."

Bas grinned. "I already have everything I could

possibly want. I have you, and I have a wonderful family. What else could you give me that could make it any better?"

Eva smiled and then pressed her lips to his. She trailed her fingers over his handsome face and said, "How about a baby?"

His expression fell from his face for a brief moment, then his lips tilted upward into a smile so full of happiness it almost hurt to gaze upon it. He lifted her wrapped her into his arms, stood, and swung her around with pure joy. "I love you so much," he said.

"I love you too," she said in a husky tone.

This was what life should be. Love and joy—even in the small moments. She only hoped that his friends, and family found the same joy in their own lives. Then everything would be perfect...

Thank you so much for taking the time to read my book.

Your opinion matters!

Please take a moment to review this book on your favorite review site and share your opinion with fellow readers.

www.authordawnbrower.com

Excerpt: A Wallflower Under the Mistletoe

DAWN BROWER

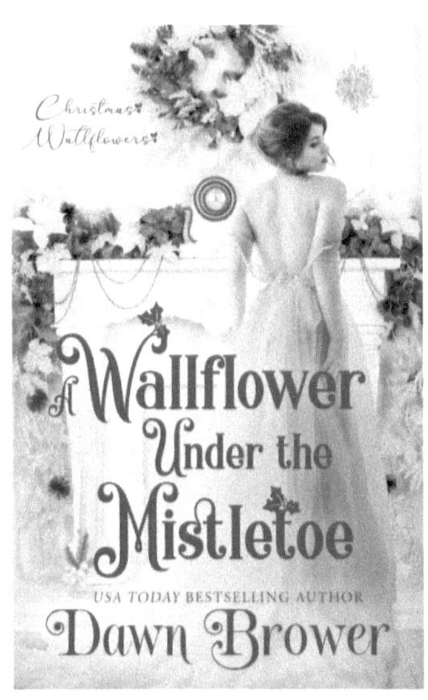

Miss Agatha Cartwright stared out the window watching snow fall from the sky. It had been snowing for several minutes, and a small white blanket had started to form on the cold ground. She turned away from the window and glanced around her tiny bedchamber. It was a sparse room. Her father, Baron Cartwright, had not believed in living frivolously. She had no creature comforts. Sometimes she thought she was lucky to have a blanket to keep her warm at night. If clothing hadn't been a necessity that might have been denied to her too.

This room spoke volumes about the lifestyle she'd had to live. There were not decorations filling the room. The walls were stark white, and the floor a polished wood that had seen better days. The floorboards were dark and needed to be replaced. Her bed was only big enough to fit her small frame. The blanket was a patchwork creation made from old clothes that could no longer be worn. She'd made it herself—so she supposed she wouldn't have that if she hadn't learned to sew with some of the ladies at the vicarage.

Her mother had died in childbed. Agatha had never known her. Perhaps if she had lived there would have been more kindness in her life. Now at four and ten, she had to leave everything she'd known, but she supposed that might be for the best. Nothing in her home had been welcoming. The baron had never liked her, and didn't keep those feelings to himself. He told her often that she was a worthless child that should have died with her mother that day.

She feared he might end her life, and that he secretly hoped she take ill and die to save him the trouble. The irony was that happened to the baron instead. He caught a random fever and died less than a sennight later. Now she was an orphan, and had no one to see to her care. What would happen to her? She couldn't stay in her home any longer. The new baron would take over the household soon and then she'd be homeless. He wouldn't want to care of her…

Agatha had always felt alone in the world. So this didn't change much, but it still hurt to accept it. If she were older perhaps it wouldn't terrify her as much. No, that was a lie. It would not matter what age she was, the unknown would always frighten her. She hated surprises, and she especially disliked not having any control in her life. She would find a way through this, and she made a vow to herself. One day she would do as she pleased and no one would ever tell her what to do again.

"Miss Agatha," a maid said from behind her.

The servants had always been nice to her. They understood her better than anyone else had. Her father had treated them better than he ever did her. So they tried to make up for his horrid behavior. They couldn't do much though. At least they never beat her. "Yes, Beth?" Agatha asked.

"There is a gentleman here to see you." She fidgeted in the doorway. "A fancy one."

Agatha pushed her eyebrows together. Who could possibly be there to see her? She didn't socialize except at church or on the days her father forced her to volunteer with the poor. "Did he tell you why he is here?" or who he was?

"He didn't," she said. "He insisted on seeing you."

She didn't want to meet with him. Agatha had learned a long time ago that stalling the inevitable never solved anything though. It was best to get the unpleasantness out of the way and move forward. "Where is he now?"

"He's in the blue salon," she said. "Should I bring tea?"

Agatha shook her head. If they served refreshments the gentleman might stay longer than she wished him too. Besides she shouldn't offer what didn't truly belong to her. She had her clothes, and the quilt she'd sewn herself. Nothing else was hers. "I do not believe that will be necessary." Agatha moved away from the window. "I'll see him now."

"Yes, miss," Beth said, then left her alone.

She glanced out the window one last time, then left her bedchamber. There was no comfort in there anyway. She doubted she'd know comfort if it bit her. And what a thought that was… A bite would be unpleasant at best. What did that say about her that she'd compared comfort to it? That she had an acerbic view on life? She supposed she did.

If she was going to meet with a fancy gentleman she should make herself presentable. She sat at her sitting table and squinted to check her appearance in the looking glass. It was small and cracked, but serviceable. Her dark hair was pinned back but a few strands had escaped the pins. She tucked them back into place. Dark circles rimmed her green eyes making the color pop against her pale skin.

She didn't look that attractive, but she never had. Agatha had put off this meeting long enough. She stood and left her bedchamber and headed toward the salon. A gentleman was indeed there waiting. He wore all black, from his breaches, to his waistcoat and jacket. His hair was dark too, and his eyes a similar shade as hers. She didn't make much of that. Agatha had always favored her mother from what she'd been told. That was one of the reasons her father hated her. She reminded him of what he'd lost. "Hello, my lord," she said and curtsied. "What may I do for you?"

He frowned and glanced at her as if he were trying to understand her. His gaze met hers and he tilted his head to the side. "Do you like living here?" he asked.

How was she to answer that? Should she speak the truth or tell him what most thought she should say? She chose to be honest. "Not particularly. Why do you ask?"

He grinned. "You're cheeky," he said.

She waited. Agatha had never spoken out of turn before. She expected a dressing down of some sort but none came. "Should I act in a different manner?" She was testing the man and didn't understand why she felt as if she could.

"I expect you to be yourself," he said. "But there are times when a person must be more circumspect. Do you know the difference?"

Agatha considered what he was asking her. "Some social niceties should be observed, but not at the risk of destroying a part of myself."

He nodded. "I've come to take you home with me. I couldn't before your father died," he began. "He would never have allowed it, but I promised your mother I would always look after you. Until now I haven't been able to keep that promise to her. I want to see it right."

"Why would you do that?"

"Because your mother has always been important to me," he answered honestly. "I'm the Duke of Wharton, and from this moment on I'll be your guardian. I have a daughter and I wouldn't want her to be left alone in the world." He waited a moment. "You don't have to live at my estate if you don't wish to. I can make other arrangements if you prefer."

He was a duke… He had to have an enormous estate. "Where would I go instead?" She should know what other choices she had before she made a decision.

"A boarding school," he told her. "Even young ladies should be educated, and I suspect your father didn't believe that. Do you read?"

She shook her head. "Father didn't bother with any sort of education." Her father barely did the smallest things for her. Education was so far above that…

"Then either way we will rectify that and see you learn everything you should, or want to." He smiled. "What would you like to do Miss Agatha?"

She considered everything he'd said. What did she want to do? She might have more freedom if she were to go away to school. That didn't sound like she'd enjoy it though. "Will I have my own room at your estate?" She thought about the barren room she'd had for her entire life.

"You'll have a room in the same wing as my daughter, Seraphina," he told her. "You'll take lessons with her once your education is caught up to hers, and we will have new clothes made for you. Whatever you decide that will be one of my priorities." He glanced over her dress. "That gown has seen better days."

Agatha had repaired it several times already… She jutted her chin out and met his gaze. "I think I'd prefer going to your estate." She hoped she didn't regret that decision. His daughter might be horrid and make Agatha's life miserable.

"Wonderful," he said. "Then we shall depart immediately. Is there anything you wish to pack? Is all of your gowns so threadbare?"

She only had one other gown, and it was far worse. "Yes, Your Grace." Now that she knew he was a duke she addressed him properly. "All my clothing is like this. I only have one item I wish to gather from my room if that is all right." It was a miniature of her mother that she'd hidden away.

"Go retrieve it. I'll wait for you." The duke nodded at her.

Agatha rushed up to her bedchamber and gathered the miniature and put it in her pocket. Then as an afterthought she took her quilt too. She didn't want the duke to know about the miniature, and the quilt would hide that fact from him. The miniature was her little secret. Perhaps one day she'd share it with someone else, but that day was not now. She folded the quilt and went back to the salon.

The duke met her gaze. "Is that all you wish to bring with you?"

She nodded. "I'm ready to depart now."

"The let's be off. It's several days ride by carriage to the estate," he told her. "Then when the season opens I must return to London. You and Seraphina will accompany me."

She'd never been to London… Agatha had a new life ahead of her and she didn't know what to think about it all. "That sounds…lovely."

They went to the duke's carriage and he helped her inside. It was cold and she was grateful she'd grabbed the quilt. She unfolded it and wrapped herself inside of it and settled into her seat. Not long after that she fell asleep, content for the first time in her life.

Two years later…

AGATHA SAT IN THE LIBRARY READING ONE OF HER favorite books. In the two years since she'd come to live with the Duke of Wharton her education had helped her learn a lot about herself. She had many interests now. She loved learning about history and geography. She read many travel books that outlined exotic lands and the animals that lived there. If she could, she'd travel the world and explore it all—if only she'd been born a man and given the freedom to do as she pleased.

The duke had taken care of everything she could possibly need. He had even set up a dowry for her. When Seraphina was launched into society, Agatha would be too. She had no desire to marry any man. The duke had told her if after three seasons she still felt that way he would allow her to travel as she liked—with a proper escort. Agatha lived for that day and studied everything she could. But not everything she read was for preparation for what she believed would be an inevitability. She also read books for pleasure—like the one she read now.

"There you are," Seraphina said from the doorway. Her red hair was plaited elegantly on top of her head. Seraphina was six months younger than Agatha, but she hadn't suffered one day in her life. She hadn't understood how to relate to Agatha at first, but she had tried and that mattered to her. They were as close as sisters now.

"I haven't been hiding," she said. "Did you need me for something?"

"Bas is here," Seraphina said. She wrinkled her nose. "And he's brought friends."

Bas—Sebastian Gray, the Earl of Somerset, was Seraphina's cousin. He'd come to live with the duke at a young age—he was several years older than Seraphina and Agatha. Though most of the time he had been away at school. Now though, he was home more often than not. He had finished all the schooling years ago and hadn't bothered with college. Eton hadn't been enjoyable for him and learning had been difficult.

"Not them…" Agatha wrinkled her nose.

Bas had two friends, the Duke of Riverdale and Marquess of Huntington. Those two were constantly with Bas, and the duke tended to irritate Seraphina. They did not get along well at all. Agatha was secretly glad they were there though. She liked both young gentlemen and they humored her. Agatha tended to ask a lot of questions and most men wouldn't deign to answer her.

"Yes, them," Seraphina said. "Please come with me. Father ordered me to be nice and entertain them." She rolled her eyes. "As if they need me to be there."

Agatha placed a ribbon in her book and closed it, then set it on a nearby table. She could always read later. Seraphina needed her. "Of course I'll come with you." She smiled at her. "Where are we going?"

"To the game room." She frowned. "They wish to play charades of all things. I hate charades."

Agatha didn't particularly like it either. "Perhaps we can suggest a different sort of entertainment…"

"I'll let you make the suggestions. They're more likely to listen to you, then me."

"Very well," Agatha agreed. "I'll think of something."

They entered the game room. The three young gentlemen were already there. Two of them were at the billiards table. Bas and Riverdale were engrossed in a game. Riverdale glanced up and glared at Seraphina. "Did you make time out of your busy schedule to grace us with your presence?" he asked.

"I would never be so rude," Seraphina said. "If I promised to do something I wouldn't ignore it for your sake, your grace."

Agatha had to step in before this took a bad turn. It was already heading in the wrong direction. "The Duke of Wharton asked us to join you for some entertainments. But if you wish for us to leave…"

"Don't be ridiculous," Bas said. "We would never ask you to leave. Come join us." Riverdale glared in his direction, but Bas either pretended not to see him or didn't care.

Agatha sighed and spared a glance at Seraphina. "I thought they wanted to play charades."

"That was father's suggestion," she admitted not at all sounding repentant either.

"Why don't we do something a little more interesting," Huntington said. He had a wicked gleam in his eyes.

Agatha had forgotten he was there, but she had always tried to ignore his presence as much as possible. She glanced in his direction and sucked in a breath. He was as gorgeous as she remembered. She didn't want to notice, but she wasn't dead. His brown hair was streaked with gold and his eyes were a brilliant amber—the same shade as the whiskey the Duke of Wharton preferred to drink.

"What do you propose?" Agatha asked him in a neutral tone. Somehow, much to he amazement, she managed to speak without stuttering. She *hated* how he made her feel.

"A game of hide and seek," he said, then grinned. "There has to be a lot of places to hide in this castle."

"I like it," Riverdale said. "Four of us can hide, then the other one will try to find us."

"Who will be our seeker first?" Bas lifted a brow.

"I'll go first," Agatha volunteered. She didn't like the idea of this game that much. Hiding in dark places reminded her too much of her childhood and the times she'd been locked in her wardrobe. It had been one of her father's favorite punishments for her.

"No," Seraphina said. "We're not playing this." She knew what Agatha had gone through. They had no secrets from each other.

Agatha placed her hand on Seraphina's arm. "It's all right," she told her. She silently pleaded with her to not make things more difficult than they had to be.

Bas glanced between them. He seemed to see more than Agatha wanted him to. He had always been perceptive. "We should play cards instead."

"We have uneven numbers," Huntington reminded him. "It's this or charades. Pick one."

Everyone groaned. "Go hide," Agatha ordered.

"I'll give you a quarter hour until I start looking. The first of you I find has to look for the other three." She had no wish to play longer than absolutely necessary.

They all stopped arguing and left the room. No room in the castle was off limits, except the duke's private chambers. Agatha sat down and watched a nearby clock. She gave them a little extra time, but not for them. She was mentally preparing herself. Then she started wandering the halls. She started with the library because it was her favorite room. No one was in there of course. Then she walked down the connecting hallway and ended up in the ballroom. It was shrouded in darkness, but she could almost imagine what it must be like filled with candlelight and dancers. It would be magical.

She swirled around the floor as if she were waltzing with an experienced partner. She should be looking for those hiding, but she was in no hurry. She closed her eyes and twirled until she bumped into someone. Agatha gasped.

"It's all right," a gentleman said. "I have you." His voice was husky against her ear.

"Lord Huntington…" Only one man made her heart skip a beat with such efficiency.

"It seems as if you've found me," he said. He seem pleased with that outcome.

She froze. Agatha didn't know what to make of this. Had he wanted her to find him? "I…" She cleared her throat. "I think it's you that's found me."

Agatha could barely make out his face in the shadows. He smiled. "That might be true too. Either way the game is over isn't it?" Huntington stepped closer to her. Heat suffused her from head to toe.

She nodded dumbly. He confused her, but she didn't want to explore those feelings too deeply. If she did she might start hoping for something that was too far out of reach for her. She was going to travel the world, not become a marchioness. *And why had that thought popped into her stupid head?*

The Marquess of Huntington hadn't offered for her and never would. He wasn't for her either way. There was no room for silly thoughts and wishfulness. "We should go back to the game room then."

"Yes," he said. His tone held an odd edge to it, almost as if he wished he could disagree with her. "You lead the way."

She didn't argue with him. "I'm going to my chamber," she told him. It was his responsibility to locate the others. "Please give my apologies to the others. I'm not feeling well." She was feeling too much and she had to escape before those unwanted emotions overwhelmed her.

Agatha reminded herself over and over as she walked away from the marquess that he wasn't for her. If she kept telling herself that, she might make herself accept it too. Agatha was a baron's daughter. A marquess did not marry so far beneath them. She best accept that now and save herself from an inevitable broken heart.

Love Be a Lady's Charm

This Book was previously part of the Luck Be a Lady's Charm anthology. If you wish to read the other three books about Eva's cousins and their path with the rose quartz go here:

Forever My Rogue by **Amanda Mariel**
https://books2read.com/ForeverMyRogue
Wicked With You **by Stacy Reid**
https://books2read.com/WickedWithYou
Only the Valet Will Do by **Sophie Barnes**
https://books2read.com/OnlytheValetWillDo

Acknowledgments

Special thanks to Elizabeth Evans. Your encouragement and assistance with this book helped me immensely. I am grateful for all you do for me.

About Dawn Brower

USA TODAY Bestselling author, DAWN BROWER writes both historical and contemporary romance. There are always stories inside her head; she just never thought she could make them come to life. That creativity has finally found an outlet.

Growing up, she was the only girl out of six children. She raised two boys as a single mother; there is never a dull moment in her life. Reading books is her favorite hobby, and she loves all genres.

www.authordawnbrower.com
TikTok: @1DawnBrower

bookbub.com/authors/dawn-brower
facebook.com/1DawnBrower
twitter.com/1DawnBrower
instagram.com/1DawnBrower
goodreads.com/dawnbrower

Also by Dawn Brower

HISTORICAL

Stand alone:

Broken Pearl

A Wallflower's Christmas Kiss

A Gypsy's Christmas Kiss

Marsden Romances

A Flawed Jewel

A Crystal Angel

A Treasured Lily

A Sanguine Gem

A Hidden Ruby

A Discarded Pearl

Marsden Descendants

Rebellious Angel

Tempting An American Princess

How to Kiss a Debutante

Loving an America Spy

Linked Across Time

Saved by My Blackguard

Searching for My Rogue

Seduction of My Rake

Surrendering to My Spy

Spellbound by My Charmer

Stolen by My Knave

Separated from My Love

Scheming with My Duke

Secluded with My Hellion

Secrets of My Beloved

Spying on My Scoundrel

Shocked by My Vixen

Smitten with My Christmas Minx

Vision of Love

Enduring Legacy

The Legacy's Origin

Charming Her Rogue

Ever Beloved

Forever My Earl

Always My Viscount

Infinitely My Marquess

Eternally My Duke

Bluestockings Defying Rogues

When An Earl Turns Wicked

A Lady Hoyden's Secret

One Wicked Kiss

Earl In Trouble

All the Ladies Love Coventry

One Less Scandalous Earl

Confessions of a Hellion

The Vixen in Red

Lady Pear's Duke

Scandal Meets Love

Love Only Me (Amanda Mariel)

Find Me Love (Dawn Brower)

If It's Love (Amanda Mariel)

Odds of Love (Dawn Brower)

Believe In Love (Amanda Mariel)

Chance of Love (Dawn Brower)

Love and Holly (Amanda Mariel)

Love and Mistletoe (Dawn Brower

The Neverhartts

Never Defy a Vixen

Never Disregard a Wallflower

Never Dare a Hellion

Never Deceive a Bluestocking

Never Disrespect a Governess

Never Desire a Duke

CONTEMPORARY

Stand alone:

Deadly Benevolence

Snowflake Kisses

Kindred Lies

Sparkle City

Diamonds Don't Cry

Hooking a Firefly

Novak Springs

Cowgirl Fever

Dirty Proof

Unbridled Pursuit

Sensual Games

Christmas Temptation

Daring Love

Passion and Lies

Desire and Jealousy

Seduction and Betrayal

Begin Again

There You'll Be

Better as a Memory

Won't Let Go

Heart's Intent

One Heart to Give

Unveiled Hearts

Heart of the Moment

Kiss My Heart Goodbye

Heart in Waiting

Heart Lessons

A Heart Redeemed

Kismet Bay

Once Upon a Christmas

New Year Revelation

All Things Valentine

Luck At First Sight

Endless Summer Days

A Witch's Charm

All Out of Gratitude

Christmas Ever After

YOUNG ADULT FANTASY

Broken Curses

The Enchanted Princess

The Bespelled Knight

The Magical Hunt